Fun and Games at the Whacks Museum

and Other Horror Stories

Fun and Games at the Whacks Museum

and Other Horror Stories

FROM
**ALFRED HITCHCOCK
MYSTERY MAGAZINE
AND ELLERY QUEEN'S
MYSTERY MAGAZINE**

EDITED BY
CATHLEEN JORDAN

Simon & Schuster Books for Young Readers
Published by Simon & Schuster
New York   London   Toronto   Sydney   Tokyo   Singapore

SIMON & SCHUSTER BOOKS FOR YOUNG READERS
1230 Avenue of the Americas, New York, New York 10020
Copyright © 1994 by Bantam Doubleday Dell Direct, Inc.
SIMON & SCHUSTER BOOKS FOR YOUNG READERS
is a trademark of Simon & Schuster.
Book design by Paul Zakris.
Manufactured in the United States of America
10 9 8 7 6 5 4 3 2 1

Library of Congress Cataloging-in-Publication Data

Fun and games at the Whacks Museum and other horror
    stories : from Alfred Hitchcock mystery magazine and
    Ellery Queen's mystery magazine / edited by Cathleen
Jordan.
        p.   cm.
      Includes bibliographical references.
      Summary: A collection of thirteen scary stories, including
"The Witch, the Child, and the U.P.S. Fellow," "Witch and
Cousin," and "The Undertaker's Wedding."
      1. Horror tales. American.   2. Children's stories, American.
[1. Horror stories.   2. Short stories.]   I. Jordan, Cathleen.
II. Alferd Hitchcock mystery magazine.   III. Ellery Queen's
mystery magazine.
PZ5.F964 1994   [Fic]—dc20   93-34862   CIP AC
ISBN: 0-671-89005-0

Contents

Preface

The two magazines from which the stories in this book were selected are mystery magazines. That is, they contain short stories that often deal with the unraveling of a crime; we find out at the end—by means of some good detective work—who did it. Clues are involved, and the interviewing of suspects, and so on.

Mystery stories in the traditional sense don't allow for the supernatural. The detective must work with the probable, or at least the possible.

But what if . . .

However satisfying, scary, clever, surprising, and entertaining a good whodunit (or other kind of crime story) may be, there remains that "what if." What if the world weren't quite the way we have to agree it is, given the evidence? What if it were a somewhat different sort of world?

What if it *is* a somewhat different sort of world?

The worlds suggested in the following stories are thirteen writers' ideas of how stories about crime might then take shape. At *Alfred Hitchcock Mystery Magazine* and, though to a lesser extent, at *Ellery Queen's Mystery Magazine,* such stories have been added to the "regular" mystery story lists because they have entertained us and because the "what if" comes to seem rather chillingly likely. After all, we don't think we've met a ghost or a witch or a vampire yet, or encountered a puddle that leads to another world, but who can say for sure?

Just maybe all the evidence isn't in.

—CATHLEEN JORDAN, EDITOR
Alfred Hitchcock Mystery Magazine

Pouring the Foundations of a Nightmare

NINA KIRIKI HOFFMAN

You can get inside a house and walk around, look out all the windows, knock on all the walls, open all the doors. You can *know* a house.

You can't crawl inside a person.

I kept thinking my best friend Garrett and I were looking out the same eyes, seeing the same views, but we weren't, especially after we turned twelve. He changed all the furniture inside his head, threw out the stuff we did together, like skateboards and video games and costumes and comic books. I couldn't understand the stuff he put in there instead.

He had nightmares when we were little, and after he stopped having them, I started. Most of my nightmares are about dead people. Garrett's used to be, too; I know, because I made some of his nightmares up. I'd pour the foundations, and he'd build the nightmares on them. And all the time, I was telling myself something, and I didn't find out what until just lately, after I talked to Garrett's dead brother Danny.

My house is tall and gray and goes up straight from the ground to the roof. It's like a big shoe box with an attic on top. My parents and I and our housekeeper, Mrs. Garrison, live in my house. Garrett's house is yellow, and twistier; you can get lost in it. When he still lived there, it was his parents, him, and his brother Danny. Now it's a bunch of apartments, and seven people live there. Our houses stand next door to each other on one of the streets in Spores Ferry, Oregon, that has lots of trees on it, with strips taken out of the sidewalk for plants and pieces of lawn. In our neighborhood, you can ride a bike or a motorcycle through the stop sign intersections without stopping, because usually there's no traffic coming. Before the accident, I sometimes went through intersections without stopping; Garrett never went through without stopping; and Garrett's older brother Danny always went through without stopping.

We spent most of our time at Garrett's house when he was still living there. He and his parents have been gone for a year now—they moved to Florida—and I haven't been to Garrett's house since they left.

A lot of my nightmares come from Garrett's house.

We knew somebody died in Garrett's house. We heard his parents talking about it. Garrett had nightmares about it from the time he was five. One day when I was really mad at him, I made up a story about the person who died. "Her name was Mad Lucy," I said as we sat on his bed sucking stolen chocolate chips and getting brown smears on Garrett's *Mad* magazines, "and she had three children, and they all lived in the same room, and at night she would stand in the doorway and listen to them breathing apart from each other. One night she thought she couldn't hear one of the babies breathing. She got a knife and stabbed one baby. Only one of the others was breathing. She stabbed the next baby. One of them was still breathing. She stabbed the third baby, and then none of them was breathing, so she came up to *this room* and hanged herself."

I never had to tell him that story again. It got built into him. When we got on our bikes to ride to school in the morning and he had bloodshot eyes, and looked too pale, and couldn't listen or talk very well, I knew he'd dreamed about Mad Lucy again, and I felt awful. His nightmares didn't end until Danny went through an intersection on his motorcycle without stopping for the last time.

The Halloween after Danny died, I dared Garrett to visit Danny's grave with me in the cemetery, and Garrett just laughed. He said okay, he didn't care.

The night was cool and misty. The streetlights were yellow; every night looked like Halloween. Dead maple leaves had drifted against the curbs in wet, slippery heaps. The air smelled good from the wood that people were burning in their fireplaces. We rode our bikes to the cemetery and locked them to the fence, then sneaked in through a gap in the hedge. We'd passed a lot of grown-ups taking little kids trick-or-treating. Garrett and I were twelve. I had wanted to be a wolfman again this year, but he said that was stupid. "Grow up, Clark," he had said.

"Free candy, Garrett," I had said.

"It's just too stupid," he had said, and it had only been a month and a half since Danny died, so I decided not to push it. I ended up daring him to go to the graveyard instead. Maybe I was thinking if he'd only have nightmares again he'd turn back into the Garrett I knew, not this calm guy who smiled and acted mature and didn't get mad anymore. Not this guy who told me he had to stay in and do homework on Saturday nights when I asked him to go to the movies with me.

We were walking along the road in the cemetery, and everything was dark and quiet. I started thinking about all the dead people under the ground. Maybe they were mad at the living, and maybe Halloween was the one night a year when they could come up and do something about it. Maybe that fresh earth smell came from somebody digging his way up. I thought about skeleton hands poking up out of earth shadowed by moonlight on tombstones, like in the *Thriller* video. The hands would drag us down against the earth and smother us, and then we would turn into skeletons ourselves, and grab other live people. When I heard these yowls like ghouls fighting, it was me who jumped and Garrett who stayed steady. "It's all right, Clark," he said. "The dead won't hurt you."

Garrett said that.

I felt strange. All my fear just melted away, and what I had left was numbness. We never made it to Danny's grave. We turned around and left. On the way home I watched all those little ghosts and witches and vampires and werewolves and princesses and fairies running from house to house, and I thought, how stupid. Then I went to bed and had my first nightmare, full of skeleton hands reaching for me. By morning the big numb place in the middle of me had come unfrozen, and I just felt really mad because I'd missed out on all that candy. I wanted to punch Garrett.

After Garrett and his folks moved away, their house got remodeled into apartments, and a cousin showed up to live in the basement and be the landlord.

The landlord at Garrett's house looked a lot like Danny in disguise, and did all the yard work after dark. He wore a beard and glasses, and underneath it all, he looked like Danny.

I dreamed about him. In my dreams, he crept all around the house, through the bushes, rustle, rustle. He was one of those ghouls from *Night of the Living Dead,* and he wanted to eat me. I heard his fingers scrabbling on the walls, heard him twisting the knob of the front door downstairs, heard glass break in a window, imagined him coming in to get me. Maybe he'd nibble off my fingers first, then bite my face. Maybe he'd go straight for my guts, rip them out of my stomach, and suck them up like spaghetti. Every night after I turned off my light I lay in bed and worried about the guy next door. The shadows on the ceiling moved and I wanted to yell. Some nights I talked to Mom and Dad, even after they went to bed. Three times my dad went downstairs to check the windows and the doors for me and tell me everything was all right. After that he stopped checking. He just said everything was all right, go to sleep. So I went back to my room. Usually I didn't go to sleep.

One summer night, I sat in my upstairs window a couple of hours after ten o'clock lights-out and watched the guy next door weed. The air smelled like lawns being watered, and smoke from the field-burning outside the city. The yellow streetlight shone brightly on the yard next door. The landlord knelt in the flowerbed near our yard—all the flowers were closed—and pulled weeds from the earth. Not like my dad, jerking them out and cussing at them, but just pouring water on the ground, feeling down around the plants' roots, and then pulling them out gently, like he didn't want to hurt them even though he was killing them. He worked slowly. I thought, Danny wasn't like that. Danny never did anything slowly. He was always racing around like a madman.

I thought I could just watch him a while and then lie in bed and shiver all night, wondering when he was coming to get me. Or I could go out there and ask him, get it over with.

I unhooked the screen and climbed out the window onto the branch of the maple tree I had always used as an escape route before I got so scared of the landlord cousin. I sneaked down the tree as quietly as I could, but when I reached the ground and turned around, there was the cousin, sitting back on his heels, staring at me through his clear glasses.

Eat me now, I thought. I'm tired of waiting. I heard my heart in my ears, thudding like a big drum.

I looked back at my house. I wished Mom or Dad would

be at the window watching. The cousin couldn't do anything if anybody was watching, could he? But there was nobody at any of the windows in my house, just a lot of curtains with dark behind them. I looked at his house, the house I used to play in with Garrett, to see if any of the tenants was at a window. The lights were on in the back downstairs apartment, but the curtains were closed. The other three apartments were dark.

"Hi," I said.

"Hel-hello," the cousin said, his voice starting out normal and then dropping down deep. He leaned over and pulled another weed.

He wasn't acting very dangerous, but I still wished I'd remembered to bring my Swiss Army knife with me. I didn't know what to do next. I wondered what his teeth looked like. I hadn't seen him smile in the year I'd been watching him.

"Have you heard anything from Garrett?" I asked.

"What?" He sat back again and stared at me.

"Garrett," I said. "Your cousin? Used to live in your house. He was my best friend."

"No," he said, still in his deep voice. He stared at me and I stared at him. He didn't smell like rotting meat or even like garbage. He didn't have claws on his fingers, and he didn't look too strong. He was just a guy. Just a guy I'd spent a year being terrified of.

"Oh," I said. "Oh, well." I turned back to the tree and put my arms around it, ready to hug my way up to the lowest branch, and then I realized I was shaking and didn't have any strength in my arms. I let go of the tree. Nothing like failing at something important in front of a scary stranger.

"Can you get in downstairs?" he asked, and it was Danny's voice coming from behind me.

I didn't turn around. "Everything's locked," I mumbled to the tree. I had checked from the inside. Twice.

"I'll give you a boost." Then he was right behind me. I pushed my face against the bark, hugged the tree again, and waited for him to bite down on the back of my neck or tear my arms off.

"Clark," he said. He touched my shoulder. His fingers felt wet and cool through my T-shirt.

I hugged the tree as hard as I could.

"I can't help you up if you won't let go."

After a long moment I let go of the tree. Maybe that would make it easier for him to carry me off. Maybe that was why he was waiting. He'd take me into the basement and butcher me in the bathtub. I turned around and looked at his face, then thought *what have I got to lose?* reached up, and pulled his beard. It came off. I dropped it and put my hands over my mouth.

After a minute he took off his glasses and put them in his shirt pocket. Then he peeled off the mustache. He was Danny, all right.

"Are you going to eat me?" I asked through my hands.

"Nope." He leaned over, picked up the beard, and stuffed it in a pants pocket. "You going to tell on me?"

"Tell what?" I lowered my hands.

"Well, who I am, I guess. What else could you tell?"

"You're dead, and you only come out at night."

"Oh. That."

"It was all a bunch of lies, wasn't it? You're not really dead, are you? It's like a spy movie or something where you're a secret witness with a new identity, huh." I was talking too fast, hoping what I was saying was true.

He smiled. He bent and made a cup with his hands for my foot. "Go to bed, Clark," he said.

I stepped into his hands and he lifted me until I could grab the lowest branch and climb up. I sat on the branch and looked down at him. "Danny?"

"What?"

"It's a spy movie, not a horror movie, right?"

"Maybe it's a comedy." He got his beard and mustache out and pasted them back on. "Doesn't this look like a comedy?" He put on his round-framed glasses and peered up at me. "Actually, I have heard from Garrett. He's fine. He asked me about you. What do you want me to tell him?"

"I lost his address, and I miss him."

"Wait a sec. Don't go away. I'll get it for you," said Danny, and he strolled across the yard and walked down the basement steps in back.

I put my arm around the tree trunk and waited. Danny was dead and he only came out at night. Garrett knew and he never told me. What kind of best friend was that?

Danny came back and handed me a slip of paper with an address on it. I put it in my pocket. "Thanks," I said. "Are you a zombie?"

"Nope."

"A ghoul?"

"Nope. What's the difference?"

"I think zombies *are* dead people and ghouls *eat* dead people, but I'm not sure. Are you a werewolf?"

"Be real, Clark. I have to finish weeding, okay?"

"Am I even warm?"

"No," he said. "Good night." He turned around and went back to his sleeping flowers.

I climbed up the maple tree and went in through my window and then sat there, watching him work in the soft yellow light. He was Danny, and he wasn't Danny. Danny always forgot his chores, too busy off somewhere playing music or cruising, doing things I planned to do three years from now, when I got my driver's license. He looked like himself and he acted like an old man.

I hooked the screen and closed the curtains and changed into my pj's and crawled into bed. For the first time in nearly two years, I was going to sleep without nightmares. Danny was just some dead guy who weeded and watered. He told me he wouldn't eat me, and he wouldn't lie about a thing like that.

I closed my eyes. I was just falling into the whirly part of sleep where all the edges of everything you think about stretch or shrink, when I sat straight up, the fear I was so used to shocking through me. He hadn't told me what he was. Sure, he had told me he wouldn't eat me, but then, he wasn't really Danny, not the way he was acting, so how could I trust him?

I went to the window and looked out. He was loading all the weeds in a wheelbarrow. He wheeled the wheelbarrow around behind the house and dumped the weeds on a pile under a tarp. It was all very un-Danny.

I went back to bed and thought about it. It came to me presently that maybe he wasn't dead, or a ghoul, or a zombie, or anything like that. Maybe he'd turned into the scariest monster of all. A grown-up.

I lay in bed awake the whole night. If it could happen to Danny, it could happen to anybody.

The next night, I watched him again. He was using a lawnmower, the kind without a motor that makes a sound like a strong sprinkler but not as wet. My dad had one of those a long time ago and he cussed it harder than he ever cussed the car. It stopped at every clump of grass and dulled its blades on every pebble. He wrestled with it. Finally he put it out with the trash and mumbled about doctors with weird fitness prescriptions.

Danny mowed. Up, down, up, down. Every once in a while something slowed the mower; then he'd lean into the handle and push the mower over whatever was in the way. Not a single curse. He'd turned into a grown-up, and not even an interesting grown-up.

I got out the letter I'd started writing to Garrett that afternoon. "How come you didn't tell me Danny wasn't dead? It took me a year to figure it out. And if he is dead, he's the boringest dead person I ever saw."

I chewed on my pencil and glanced out the window. Danny lifted the lawnmower in one fist and strolled toward the house with it swaying back and forth like a pendulum, then glanced up at my window and dropped it. It thudded and I ducked. I reached for the light to switch it off, but it was too far away, and I knew he had seen me anyway. I huddled on the floor, feeling the fear pumping through me, wondering why I was scared. I just saw a guy drop a lawnmower, that was all. After a minute the shakes stopped, and I crept toward the lamp. It was sitting up on my desk. I lay on the floor, reached in under my desk, and yanked the plug out of the wall socket.

"Clark," whispered a voice from the direction of the window.

I froze.

"Clark?" A little louder now.

I thought about Garrett telling me dead people wouldn't hurt me. I wondered what kind of dead people they had in Florida. Old dead people, maybe, and drug smugglers. Voodoo dead people. Maybe Garrett had changed his mind by now.

"I just don't want you to worry," said Danny's voice.

I sat up and scooted in under my desk. "Worry about what?" I muttered, my voice rough around the edges.

"I'm not going to hurt you."

"You're not the real Danny. How do I know you're not lying?"

"What?"

He sounded so much like Danny—confused, a little irritated—that I peeked up over the top of my desk. His head was just outside my screen, and it was dark in my room; he was a silhouette, backlit by the streetlight. There were two red spots where his eyes should be. I screamed, not high like a girl, but just a sort of half-swallowed "Aaaaah!," then clapped my hand over my mouth.

"What?" he said. He blinked. I could tell because the red spots winked out and came back.

"Your eyes!"

"Huh?" He turned, looking toward the street, and I saw his nose outlined in yellow, and a sliver of his cheek; the light shone through his fake beard and glinted off his glasses. "Clark? Are you all right?"

"Danny," I said, hoping my saying his name would turn him into the normal boring person he had seemed like last night and earlier tonight. My mouth was dry. "Your eyes glow red in the dark."

"Darn," he said. Like he'd just gotten a popcorn hull stuck in his teeth or something.

"What are you doing up in my tree?"

"I saw you disappear and I thought maybe you fell down. I thought I'd better check. Then the light went out."

"You dropped the lawnmower. After carrying it like it weighed nothing."

"Darn. You did see that."

"Danny," I said, and it came out a muffled wail. "What are you?"

"Aw, Clark."

"You gonna suck my blood?"

"Nope."

"Are you still you at all?"

"Mostly," he said. "Just dead."

"How come you—how come you act like a little old man?"

"Is that what's bothering you?" He paused. "Clark, you'll find this out pretty soon. You've got to pretend to be a grown-up, or people ask too many questions, especially if you're running around in a big body."

"You never acted like a grown-up when you were alive. It's only since you died."

"Because now more than ever it's important for me not to make people ask questions. I have to try to look normal."

"Doing the yard work at night isn't normal."

"It's more important that the yard looks nice than that I don't do it at night. I own the building. I have to keep the neighborhood people happy; if they think I'm a bad neighbor, they'll start talking. And after they talk for a while, they might do something."

"Like find out you're a vampire?" It was my last shot. I'd been saving that one, maybe because it fitted the facts best and I didn't want it to be the truth. Of all the monsters there were, vampires scared me the most, because they had their own minds, and they still hurt people.

"I don't know if they'd find that out," said Danny, not saying if he was a vampire or not, "but they might do something legal to me, like take away my property, and I depend on having that house and the income it generates. Darn, I do sound like a grown-up." He was quiet for a long minute. "Maybe I am a grown-up."

"You can't be a grown-up," I said. I looked at the red spots floating in his head's shadow and tried to imagine his face around them. "You can't. You died before you had to be a grown-up."

"Yeah," he said after a moment, "and it didn't work."

"You can't be a grown-up and sleep in a coffin."

"Unless you're dead."

"Grown-ups don't go around sucking people's blood."

"They do it all the time. They call it something else."

"Grown-ups don't have eyes that glow red in the dark."

"You got me on that one."

I crawled up and sat on my desk, right near the window. I put my hand on the screen, and Danny touched it through the mesh. His fingers felt cool. After a minute I took my hand down and he put his down. "Honest you're not going to hurt me?" I said.

"Honest."

"I've been having bad dreams about you."

"I'm sorry. Listen, you're safe as long as you don't invite me in."

I had forgotten about that vampire rule. "Can you turn into a bat?" I asked.

"Uh-huh. Not very well yet."

"No grown-up could do that."

He was quiet for a while. He looked toward the street again. The yellow light touched the surface of his eye and covered the red glow. "Clark," he said, "growing up isn't something you can stop from happening. Not very easily, anyway. I did my best and it didn't work. You don't have to worry about it for a while. But when you do, it won't really hurt that much."

"That's what I'm afraid of," I whispered. "Waking up one day and it'll be too late. I won't have felt it happening." The nightmares were really to keep me from sleeping my way into being a grown-up.

"What's wrong with being a grown-up?"

Words came out of me, thoughts I hadn't noticed having. "There's no magic. All of a sudden everything happens because of something you can explain, and you don't have to be afraid of anything, and—" I thought about Garrett walking calmly through a cemetery on Halloween night. That was what was wrong. All of a sudden, Garrett was a grown-up, and I wasn't. He lost his nightmares.

I found mine.

"—and you don't see anything anymore." I thought about Dad, telling me everything was all right downstairs without even checking. "'Cause you're not even looking. And nothing's important, and nothing's happening right now. I've been watching Mom and Dad and people on TV, and they talk like it's all yesterday or tomorrow, how are we going to pay for this, when are we going on vacation, how could you spend that much on clothes? I'm going to turn fourteen this year. I have this nightmare where I fall asleep the night before my birthday, and when I wake up the next morning, bam! Instant grown-up."

Being a grown-up was like being dead. Skeleton hands, reaching up to smother. Drag everybody else under the ground to die and be a grown-up, too.

"I had that nightmare, too," Danny said. "It didn't happen like that."

"But it did happen, didn't it? How?"

"Oh, Clark," he said, and sighed.

"It happens when you start thinking your parents are right about everything and you worry about paying taxes and balancing the checkbook and stuff like that, right?"

"That's part of it."

"If I never, never do that, maybe it won't happen."

"I don't think that'll work. But I think—I have to think about this. There might be something . . ."

Mom knocked on my door. "Clark?" she called. "Who are you talking to? Are you listening to the radio? Why are you still awake? Go to sleep!"

I looked out the window. Danny had disappeared.

"Okay, Mom," I said. I climbed into bed and lay under the sheet, thinking about Danny. All day maybe he lay in a coffin in the basement next door. In the movies they always got all the stuff together, garlic, crosses, stake and a hammer to pound it with, and hunted out the coffins and killed the vampires like they were cockroaches. What if Danny's tenants figured out what he was? How could they not know? What if they got into his apartment and staked him out?

But they were grown-ups. They wouldn't wonder about it. They wouldn't believe it. I turned over and went to sleep.

The next night I went over to Garrett's house before bedtime, around nine fifteen, when the sun had been down for a few minutes, and sat on the basement steps. Danny, in disguise, came out a couple of minutes later. He jumped when he saw me.

"Look," I said, "I believe in you."

"I know that about you, Clark. Can we talk later? I have to go visit a couple of friends."

"No, I mean, I believe in you, and no grown-up would believe in vampires if they weren't one, would they?"

"So?"

"So as long as I believe in you, I won't be a grown-up."

He gave me a grin that showed all his teeth. They looked like normal teeth. "That's great," he said, and I almost lost it. How could he be a vampire and have normal teeth? Except for the chip on the front one; he'd had that for years. When I first asked him about it, I was six. He said he got it in a bicycle accident when he was too young to ride motorcycles. So, maybe he wasn't a vampire, and that blew my protection against being a grown-up out of the water. "I have to go, Clark," he said, and saved me again.

He turned into mist and blew away, even though there was no wind.

"Clark, it's almost bedtime," yelled my mom from the back door. "Come home and brush your teeth!"

I walked across Danny's carefully tended yard and hugged my secret. I started a new letter in my head. "Dear Garrett," it said. "Greetings from my nightmare."

As long as my house is haunted, I don't think any grown-up will move in.

Sitter

THEODORE H. HOFFMAN

It's shortly after you've checked on the kids again that you hear the first noise.

You're sitting on the couch, sipping Diet Coke. Their Diet Coke; it tastes funny, somehow. Minutes ago you'd tiptoed up the stairs, peering in on the kids, hoping the light from the hallway wouldn't disturb them. Even in such dim light you could see the bruise on little Brian's cheek. A fall, Mrs. Redgrave ("Oh, please call me Cam!") had said. But you'd watched the way Brian had held back from his parents, clinging to Samantha. None of the standard histrionics (hooray for vocabulary tests), the tears and the "don't go's." It had seemed like shyness, normal in kids when around strangers. Now you realize it was fear. Fear of Mr. Redgrave, mostly, with his marble eyes and too-moist grin. A man who wanted things his way, and was willing to use force to get them. Yes: You can see it now in your mind's eye, more clearly than when it happened, when they walked out the door ("We'll be back by eleven! Take care of our babies!") and climbed into the BMW (of course) and zipped off to their little party. Then, you had been pleased that Mrs.—Cam—had not gone through that little speech the other mothers all did, "the emergency numbers are right next to the phone" (with that distant look of suspicion in their eyes). You'd thought that meant she trusted you. Now, you understand it meant she didn't care.

The kids were terrific, just as Nance had said. Quiet kids. The kind you want to have someday. Not like some of the brats you've sat for (usually just once), not weird like in the movies where they crawl out of your womb with bloody claws and hate in their oversized brains. . . .

They'd gone to bed right when they were supposed to. You tucked them in carefully, humming to them. At five and two-and-a-half, so pure, so simple. So helpless. You'd asked Brian about that bruise, and he hesitated only a moment before echoing his mother's story about The Fall in the Front Yard. But hesitated nonetheless. What did he have to be afraid of, you'd wondered; and then Mr. Redgrave rose in your mind's eye like a vampire at dusk.

And now you've heard a noise.

—*scruff*—

Frozen, holding your breath, can of soda angled so near your lips, you strain to listen. (DDDUUUhhhnnnn . . . swells the trembling pipe organ in your head.) Nothing; even the silence is quiet, for once. You let out your breath, and wonder if you should have a look around. Check on the kids. ("Why don't you check the children," and there's Carol Kane, getting the phone call from the police telling her that those murderous, obscene phone calls have been coming from *inside the house* and the door to the kids' room is creaking open and)

(STOP IT.)

Silence. You sit back. Smiling. You're not going to be like the girls in those stupid movies, going to investigate every sound, usually with a stupid candle, and the psycho whose escape from the nuthouse you'd heard about on the radio (never never play the radio or TV while babysitting, too much chance you'll hear or see something unpleasant, stick to the cassettes, Barry Manilow and Bon Jovi), the psycho is waiting around the corner with nail clippers, waiting to do ungodly things to you. . . . Then again, there are the fools in the war movies, the sentries who hear something and shrug and go back to their card game, and wind up with an extra mouth gaping between their eyes. . . .

Darn it. (Why do you do this, why do you do this every stupid time?)

You get up. Pace. It's a lovely house, big and soft and bright. (Jack Nicholson could get lost in here, too) (now STOP it.) You listen to your breathing, settle it down, grip the can more tightly. Walk over to the photos on the fireplace mantel. Yup: the Grand Canyon (Hello! you mouth to the frozen family waving to you, Cam cradling little Brian as though to pitch him over the side). Niagara Falls (why do parents let their kids so near the rails? You can see the headlines—*dead*lines, that voice inside your head says—KID FALLS TO WATERY DEATH AS STUPID PARENTS—)

—*click*—

—now what *was* that?

You listen, stock-still, and the silence seems to be whispering now, but your mind tries to comfort you: Hey. Houses, even new ones, settle at night. Calm down. They have a cat, remember? You haven't seen it since you put the kids to bed, and it hasn't come near you, it's scared, remember? The doors and windows are locked. You've checked. Calm down.

You let out your breath. You feel it empty from your lungs, inflate your cheeks, rush over your lips; and you do it again just to replay the feeling. There's something reassuring about it. (Yeah—the dead can't breathe) (oh now just STOP it!)

Quiet.

Quiet.

(TOO quiet, your mind says, and you think SHUT UP! and your mind does, angrily and reluctantly.) You realize you are in a vulnerable position. They could come from so many directions. From the hallway to your left. From behind the wall obscuring most of the foyer, which leads to the kitchen. (Is that where the sounds are coming from? The kitchen?) (. . . knives . . .) (TOLD YOU TO SHUT UP!) From the window behind you, with that flimsy lock you keep checking. From the fireplace. (THE SANTA CLAUS MURDERS, the deadline screams, and they get Jamie Lee Curtis to play you in the movie and it's called *Santa Claws,* and at the climax there's a slayride, and

SITTER   31

there's Jamie Lee on the living room floor with her face sheared off and the blood isn't pouring or spurting it's *bubbling* like when you blow through a straw into a strawberry shake, and out in the woods the masked killer is cupping your face in his hands and it's still alive, your eyes blinking and your mouth trying to form words, and he's leaning to kiss you with his leathery wet lips and his tongue curls inside your mouth, licking his palms, and HIS EYES ARE MR. REDGRAVE'S) and there's a pounding, someone at the door? behind the wall? upstairs in the kids' bedroom (oh no not there, anywhere but there) . . . ? And you whirl around before you realize the pounding is your heart, just seventeen years old and trying to work itself into a coronary (like Daddy's and—DARN IT—*he* lived). . . .

—*Scruff.*

You hear it. It's not like the other times, the other houses. You *know* you hear it. You still don't know what it is—your mind's not even goading you with guesses anymore—but it is a noise and it seems to be coming from the kitchen and it is caused by something. *Some*thing. (Or some *thing*, that voice adds, smiling wickedly, but you expected it to say that) and you shake your head and, aloud, say, "No."

The sound is swallowed by the house, tasted, passed quickly from corner to corner, room to room, chair to rug to banister to front door. "No." You hear it whispered hungrily around you; and you know you do not hear it, and you listen until it fades away.

In that eye of stillness, you do what you always do, what you must do. You devise escape routes. Contingencies;

that's what they're called in those war movies. You consider every scenario (now where'd you get *that* word?) and work out an escape. If they come through that window—and you edge over to check the lock again; yes—then you'll LEAP OVER THE SOFA, FLINGING THE LAMP BEHIND YOU WITH YOUR LEFT ARM, AND HEAD FOR THE STAIRS, GRABBING THE VASE AS YOU RUN, YELLING BLOODY MURDER (what a stupid phrase), YELLING LIKE MAD AS YOU RUN, READY TO DO WHATEVER YOU HAVE TO DO TO SAVE THE CHILDREN. . . .

And you feel better as you stand there, working out escape routes. Refusing to hear any more noises. You roll your shoulders, flex your fingers, stretch. Not much longer now. The Redgraves, whatever their other problems, are a prompt couple; that's what Nance told you, anyway.

But then you'd probably have taken the job no matter what she told you (like about Mr. Redgrave's eyes and lips). Because you've missed it. Babysitting. After that last time, word has gotten around, and none of the mothers call you anymore. That bothers you, how mothers can be so stupid, that they can't see how you'd give your life to protect their kids (something your parents would never do). Anything you'd done was done with their precious little children in mind—most of them brats anyway. Not like these kids, Brian and Samantha. They're so . . . vulnerable. And having to grow up with that ugly name. Redgrave—sounds like where Communist vampires come from. (Mr. Redgrave rises in your mind again, teeth bared now.) These lousy parents couldn't even get their *name* right.

Or their house. You hug yourself, looking around slowly. Too big, too empty. Why don't they have an alarm system? This may be a nice neighborhood, not much riffraff (now you're talking like Daddy); but still, this is the kind of place you'd think the really good burglars would try to hit, especially on such a big lot, fenced in so the neighbors can't see in (OH WHY DO YOU DO THIS TO YOURSELF EVERY, SINGLE, TIME?). You are getting mad. Less and less at that stupid voice in your head, more and more at the Redgraves. Running off to their little social functions, leaving these sweet kids with strangers and bruises. (Nance has already sat for these people *six times* since they moved in. And she may be a terrific friend—she got you this job, didn't she?—but you *know* she doesn't care about the kids as much as you do. She wouldn't put her life on the line for them. She can't even keep her eyes open for half of the best moments in the horror movies you take her to!) You smile, and wonder if there is a gun in the house—

Click.

—and your nerves are shrieking again, your mind racing (what the heck is that what the heck *is* that!). "*Scruff click?*" What makes a noise like that, you wonder, backing from the entrance leading to the kitchen, where the sounds are definitely coming from. What? Maybe the cat eating from a dish? One of the kids sneaking a midnight snack? (Oh no, is it really that late?—No, no, just ten forty-five, hold on, hold on, they'll be back by no later than eleven, that's what Cam said, "no later than eleven," that's what she promised. . . .) Maybe the refrigerator coming on? Maybe a hooded strangler easing the window open with blood-bloated eyes (Mr. Redgrave's eyes) and piano wire in his raw meaty hands and . . .

(STOP THIS RIGHT NOW!)

. . . and you realize you are pacing the room, choking a pillow from the couch, walking dangerously near those entranceways. . . . You take an angry breath, and you turn as though to march right into that kitchen and prove to yourself that it's just happening again (memories flare in your mind like those flashing lights on the police cars), you're overreacting to your stupid imagination, just like Daddy says, you're being silly, inventing murderers and monsters, probably inventing the noises—

Scruff click

—*no you're not.*

The phone. You back to it, trying to swallow, ready to throw the pillow and go for the andirons or whatever the heck you call those fireplace pole things—

And suddenly you see yourself in your mind. It's like a movie. The way the sounds come just at the most quiet moments. The way the house is set behind dark fences. The stairs (*Psycho* . . .). The kids ("Why don't you check the children," and was his name really Brian or was it Damian, is she really Baby Jane . . . ?) (JUST SHUT UP!) No alarms. No emergency numbers. Redgraves. Red. Graves. Eyes and lips. Bruises.

You reach for the pole (poker, a poker, that's what it's called, CALM DOWN), and it feels oh so solid in your hand; yet it accelerates your fear, because holding it means you're serious, you really think there's somebody in the house and you've really got a weapon in your hand and you've really, finally, got to protect the children. . . .

Scrick.

Your free hand wavers over the phone. You *can't* call the police. What if it is (but you KNOW it's not) another false alarm? You can't stand the thought of everyone looking at you again, like they're scared of you; or making fun of you like those creeps in school. More lectures from Daddy, even Nance acting different around you . . .

No. Hold on. "No later than eleven," and that means she thinks they'll probably get home BEFORE then, and it's nearly eleven now, and there's just not enough time for someone to be stabbed strangled butchered (SHUT UP) raped burned (PLEASE SHUT UP!) . . . .

Nance. She's home. (Thank goodness for grounding! Bless you, Mr. Piper, you jerk!) And you pick up the receiver and start dialing, awkwardly holding the poker with your little finger against your palm.

—*SCRUFF*—

and ignoring the noises

—*CLICK*—

and when the cat runs in, an orange blur, you can't help it you SCREAM—Jamie Lee Curtis could *never* duplicate that—and the darn cat changes its mind and heads right on back out of there!

And it's all so silly and stupid that you laugh, just the way the script would say to do; and you look at the poker you've somehow held onto and you feel—moronic, a scared little schoolgirl (and hoping you didn't wake the kids). You toss the poker onto the plush rug the way the girl always does in the movies, and it lands so softly, as softly as the footstep behind you as the hand that covers your mouth as the hand that wraps around the phone receiver warm and hairy, and almost as softly as the chillingly familiar voice that says, "That's a good girl," then stays quiet no matter what those terrible hands are doing. . . .

. . . except . . .

Except:

Before any of that can happen you get your hand around the back of his head (his breath in your ear is so *hot*) and you grab a handful of mask and the hair beneath it and YANK and somehow he's flying over your shoulder, you hear him gasp and his painful grip is gone; and before he can even land you're leaping over the couch, flinging the lamp behind you with your left arm, and heading for the stairs, grabbing the vase as you run; and you are about to scream because you hear him thundering up behind you, thundering through the plush silence of the rug with certain murder in his eyes (oh how you know those eyes) but he's got to get by you to get at the children so you raise the vase and turn to brain him . . .

No one.

You let your breath run wild and glance around madly (where is he where *is* he?); and you jerk around because maybe somehow he got on the stairs above you, but no one—

—and somehow it's worse, not being able to see him, not knowing where he is (even though you know WHO he is), waiting for him to JUMP OUT AT YOU KNIFE RAISED TEETH BARED and chills and shivers rack you, you stab out a hand to turn on the lamp next to the stairs, and the light chases the shadows; and you feel a stirring of triumph, because he can't get you in the light; these psychos need the darkness, and you skitter through the room, vase at the ready, and turn on every light you can!

And you catch your breath. Your thoughts. Survey the situation. Form your escape routes. And somehow you know he is going to try to do the unexpected; going to try to get at you through the least likely way.

The front door. (The last thing you'd ever suspect.) (HA!)

You gather what's left of your courage and let it propel you into the living room again, to the poker. It seems to jump into your hand. You toss the vase onto the couch (so quietly it bounces . . .).

You're ready.

A calm fills you. A sense of confidence. Of justice. You take your place behind the front door, away from the window that would give you away. The poker is firm in your grasp. You're *not* going to be like one of those girls in the movies. You're *prepared.* Your escape routes are *planned.* You glance at the stairs—the way the psycho would get at those lovely kids. You won't let that happen. They're going to make it. So are you. As the glare of headlights cuts through the window, you steady yourself, and raise the poker.

—And in the breathless silence, there is another voice.

The voice you have heard so many times before, at moments like this. A calm voice, soothing yet insistent. The poker wavers.

(No. Not yet. Not here. Not them.)

Distantly, you hear a car door slam. Light laughter.

(Yes. The poker down. Softly, hurry. Back in its place. Yes.)

The muffled rhythm of shoes on a driveway.

(Quickly. Lights, off. The vase. Good. The lamp. Yes. Everything is all right. Remember always your ultimate escape route: the appearance of normality. Never let them know what happens behind these eyes.)

The rustle of a key, struggling to fill a lock.

(The time will come. Patience.)

You are sitting on the sofa, finishing the Diet Coke when the door opens. You look up, and smile. Cam smiles back. So does Mr. Redgrave. And you see how much, in this light, he looks like Daddy.

"Well! Here we are, right on time! Everything go okay? Samantha or Brian give you any trouble?" Cam asks, handing her wrap to Mr. Redgrave, looking around the room.

"Not a bit," you say, standing. Walking toward them, over that mute rug. "Straight to bed, and right on time. They're lovely children—Cam."

She smiles, lightly squeezes your shoulder. "Well, thank you. And from what I can see, Nancy was right: You are a very sweet and dependable young woman. Don't you think, David?"

"Looks that way," he says, and looms over you for a moment. "Looks as though you've certainly earned your money. Cam and I are grateful. Well, suppose I should get you home. Got everything?"

(Yes.)

As you get your purse, you wonder if you should ask to see the children one more time, to make sure they are okay. Their faces dance in your mind briefly (like sugarplums), and you glance around to make sure the shadows hiding at the corners of the room are empty.

"Ready," you say.

(Yes . . .)

Cam waves. "We'll let you know when we need you again, honey—"

(. . . soon . . .)

"—and, really, thank you again. You'll hear from us soon. I'm afraid poor Nancy may have talked herself out of a job!"

(. . . YES . . .)

You follow him to the car. He even opens the door for you. As you sit back in the soft seat, he says, "There's a concert next week Cam and I were planning to attend. Are you doing anything Wednesday night?"

You close your eyes. Smile. "Not a thing." And you wait for the screen to fade to black.

The Three D's

Ogden Nash

Victoria was an attractive new girl at the Misses Mallisons' Female Seminary—such an attractive new girl, indeed, that it is a pity she never grew to be an old girl. Perhaps she would have, if the Misses Mallison had established their seminary a little closer to Newburyport—or at least a little farther from Salem.

Victoria was good enough at games and not too good at lessons; her mouth was wide enough to console the homely girls and her eyes bright enough to include her among the pretty ones; she could weep over the death of a horse in a story and remain composed at the death of an aunt in the hospital; she would rather eat between meals than at them; she wrote to her parents once a week if in need of anything; and she truly meant to do the right thing, only so often doing the wrong thing was easier.

In short, Victoria was an ideal candidate for The Three D's, that night-blooming sorority which had, like the cereus, flourished after dark for many years, unscented by the precise noses of the Misses Mallison.

So felt The Three D's, so felt Victoria, and the only obstacle to her admission lay in the very title of the club itself, which members knew signified that none could gain entrance without the accomplishment of a feat Daring, Deadly, and Done-never-before. Victoria was competent at daring feats, unsurpassable at deadly feats, but where was she to discover a feat done-never-before?

Of the present membership, Amanda had leaped into a cold bath with her clothes on, Miranda had climbed the roof in her nightgown to drop a garter snake down the Misses Mallisons' chimney, Amelia had eaten cold spaghetti blindfolded thinking it was worms, and Cordelia had eaten worms blindfolded thinking they were cold spaghetti. What was left for Victoria?

It was Amanda who, at a meeting of the steering committee, wiped the fudge from her fingers on the inside of her dressing gown and spoke the name of Eliza Catspaugh.

"Who was she?" asked Miranda, pouring honey on a slice of coconut cake.

"A witch," said Amanda.

"She was burned," said Amelia.

"Hanged," said Cordelia.

"And she couldn't get into the churchyard, so they buried her in the meadow behind the old slaughterhouse," said Amanda.

"The gravestone is still there," said Amelia. "Oh, bother, the cake's all gone! Never mind, I'll eat caramels."

"There's writing on it, too," said Cordelia, who was not hungry, "but you can't read it in the daytime, only by moonlight."

"I'd forgotten how good currant jelly is on marshmallows," said Amanda. "The Three D's must tell Victoria about Eliza Catspaugh."

Late next evening Victoria took her pen in hand. *Dear Father and Mother,* she wrote, *I hope you are well. I am doing well in algebra but Miss Hattie is unfair about my French ireguler verbs. I am doing well in grammar but Miss Mettie has choosen me to pick on. Dear Father, everybody elses Father sends them one dollar every week. I have lots of things to write but the bell is wringing for supper. Lots of love, your loveing daughter, Victoria.*

Victoria knew that in ten minutes Miss Hattie Mallison would open the door slightly, peer at the bed, murmur, "Good night, Victoria, sweet dreams," and disappear. It took Victoria seven minutes to construct a dummy out of a mop, a nightgown, and several pillows and blankets. As she lowered herself to the ground she heard the door open, heard Miss Hattie's murmur, heard the door close.

The soaring moon ran through Victoria as she marched, as she skipped, as she pranced toward the old slaughterhouse. She had for company her high moon-spirits and her long shadow—the shadow which was a Victoria that no Miss Mallison could ever cage. No girl has ever had a taller, livelier companion than my shadow, thought

Victoria, and she breathed deeply and spread her arms, and her shadow breathed with her and spread crooked arms up the walls and across the roof of the slaughterhouse.

The moon grew brighter with each burr that Victoria struggled against on her way across the meadow that had been abandoned to burrs, the meadow where no beasts fed, the meadow where Victoria's shadow strengthened at each proud and adventurous step.

Where the burrs grew thickest, where her loyalty to The Three D's wore the thinnest, she came upon the gravestone. How hard the moon shone as Victoria leaned against the crooked slab, perhaps to catch her breath, perhaps to stand on one foot and pluck the burrs off. When the stone quivered and rocked behind her, and the ground trembled beneath her feet, she bravely remembered her purpose: that at midnight, in the moonlight, she was to prove herself a worthy companion of Amanda and Miranda, Amelia and Cordelia. Unwillingly she turned, and willfully she read the lines which the rays of the moon lifted from the stone so obscured by rain and moss.

Here Waits
ELIZA CATSPAUGH
Who touches this stone
on moonlight meadow
shall live no longer
than his shadow.

The job of memorizing was done, the initiation into The Three D's handsomely undergone. Gracious, is that all there is to it? thought Victoria, and set out for the seminary.

It was natural that she should hurry, so perhaps it was

natural that she did not miss the exuberant shadow which should have escorted her home. The moon was bright behind Victoria—who can tell how she forgot there should have been a shadow to lead the way?

But there was no shadow—her shadow had dwindled as she ran, as though Victoria grew shorter, or perhaps the moon grew more remote. And if she did not miss her shadow, neither did she hear or see whatever it may have been that rustled and scuttled past her and ahead of her.

I hope my dear little dummy is still there, thought Victoria as she climbed through the window. I hope Miss Hattie hasn't been unfair and shaken me.

She tiptoed across the room in the dark to the bed and bent to remove the dummy. But as she reached down, the dummy, which was no longer a dummy, reached up its dusty fingers first . . .

The Witch, the Child, and the U.P.S. Fellow

ALAN RYAN

Once upon a time (although, really, it wasn't all that long ago) in a land far away (although, if the truth be known, it wasn't nearly so far away as you might think) there lived a very old witch. She was old as only the witchiest of witches can grow old—older, in fact, than the proverbial hills, older even than the primordial slime that gave form to the hills in the first place. And what a sight she was to behold: bent nearly in half, misshapen, bow-legged (Curse that blasted broom! She had lately taken to riding the thing sidesaddle, when she could bear to ride it at all, which wasn't very often anymore, her arthritis being what it was, and sidesaddle not being the safest posture anyway for broom-riding, she had taken more than a few nasty spills, once landing wrong end up in a warm chimney, her skirts around her ears and her bloomers flapping for all the world to see, at least as much of the world as was up and about at that hour of the night), and with all the usual unsightly warts on her nose beyond the power of even the most skillful dermatologist to vanquish. Oh, yes, and snaggle teeth. It would be a mistake to forget the snaggle teeth. She was always very touchy on that point whenever anyone took a notion to write her up. She mayn't have been a beauty, but she was very particular.

This old witch of whom we speak lived—this isn't likely to come as any terrific surprise—in a most unusual sort of a house. Far be it for her to make her dwelling in anything smacking of the usual. No way, not her! The real estate agent had offered her the ever-popular gingerbread model, but she'd turned it down flat. Instead, she had a house made of dried cabbage leaves and stale bagels and various odds and ends of cafeteria foods, otherwise unidentified, and the cracks in the walls were pretty effectively stopped up with pages torn from old grammar textbooks which, the old witch firmly believed, would pretty much stop up anything or anybody, much less a vagrant breeze. The house was ugly but it was snug.

She had lived alone in the house for years and years and, since she was never inclined to extend herself very much in the direction of hospitality, no living soul had ever set foot in the house.

Even the otherwise friendly fellow who drove the U.P.S. truck on the route that served her house—a fellow perfectly willing to stop by at other houses for a short while on a chilly, damp day to enjoy a warming cup of cocoa or other refreshment tendered by a kindly-hearted house-wife—refused to venture so much as a toe past the rickety old gate that hung from a single rusty hinge in a badly weathered fence. Beyond it, an unused and largely over-grown path led from the road to the door of the house. The U.P.S. fellow would just drive up, stop his truck opposite the gate, say "Toot, toot!" very loud a couple of times, then dump the packages—marked "perishable," every single one of them—on the weedy ground by the gate. He knew the witch was old and unsteady on her feet, and ordinarily he would have been quite willing to carry the parcels right up to the house (as the company's rules actually required) but, no sir, not in this case. He had once, you see, acci-dentally dropped one of the packages. The side had split open and the contents, from the look of them, seemed to have quite perished already, although they were still mak-ing a pretty good show of squiggling around under their own steam. After that, the fellow had to grit his teeth just to lift the parcels from the truck and deposit them swiftly on the ground by the gate. Then he'd just toot a few times and drive off, and that old witch could just flit down to the gate on her broom and flit right back on up to the house with the packages tucked under her arm, for all he cared.

The neighbors, of course, had given up coming to call hundreds of years before. When people get the cold shoul-der too many times, even the sturdiest of welcome wagons breaks down.

So the old witch lived in solitary splendor and she liked it just fine, she did.

And then everything changed.

*   *   *

The day everything changed was going along, until it happened, pretty much like any other day. The tattered curtains were drawn across the grimy windows to keep out the sunlight, the cat was yowling piteously in the cellar (a long, drawn out "Meooooow!"), the grayed sheets sagged silently and sadly across the bulky outlines of the anti-quated furniture, and from time to time, just for good mea-sure, a floorboard uttered a snap or a groan quite of its own accord, as if eager to keep up its end of things. The old witch, as was her custom, was doing the housework, which consisted mainly of scattering a new layer of dust on the sideboard and stirring some greasy concoction on the stove. Quite an ordinary day, and the witch was content-edly humming a favorite cackle as she worked.

Then the doorbell chimed.

The witch jumped at the unexpected sound and, in her fluster, accidentally dropped an extra handful of dust into the stewpot she was stirring.

In the cellar, the cat cried, "Meooooow!"

The witch's surprise (and the cat's too, for that matter) can best be understood by reflecting on the fact that, as near as can be calculated from the evidence available, no one had come calling for several centuries, always except-ing the U.P.S. fellow who, as we've already noted, confined himself to tooting in the road and never actually came up to the door. (It might also be noted in passing, and in the interests of accuracy, that the doorbell didn't actually chime, properly speaking. In truth, the sound it made was more on the order of a dry rattle, rather like the sound made by a handful of bleached bones being rubbed vigorously together. It was a curious device, devilishly clever, but there's no need to dwell further on it here.)

Then, before the old witch had quite recovered from the first surprise, the doorbell chimed—or rattled—again.

"Blast!" the witch muttered. (Her snaggle teeth made it come out more like "Blatht," but we'll let it pass for now.) "Who in blazes could that be?" Eyes fixed on the door and head cocked alertly to one side (an awkward and painful posture for a witch of her years, but custom, after all, is custom), she slowly hobbled across the single small room of the house. Only when she reached the door and actually grasped the handle with her gnarled fingers did she hesitate.

"Who's there?" she cried out.

"Me," said a tiny whisper of a voice, barely audible, on the other side of the door.

"Oh," said the witch. She was, remember, quite startled to begin with and she had little or no experience in dealing with callers, so the situation already had her totally flummoxed. Before she could gather her wits safely about her like a shroud, her bony fingers had plucked at the door handle. Hinges squealing, the door swung partially open.

The witch was so taken aback by what she saw on her doorstep that she ignored the bright rays of the sun that struck her full in her withered face.

"Ach!" she cried, or words to that effect.

There on the doorstep stood the prettiest little girl in all the world. It would be misleading, of course, to say that she was the prettiest little girl the witch had ever seen in all her long life because, naturally enough, the witch was hardly in the habit of entertaining little girls. Even if she was, her preference would have gone every time to the ugly ones, and the pretty ones could fend for themselves and welcome to it. But, in any case, the old witch had no experience whatever with little girls, pretty or otherwise, and she was so thrown off balance by the sight of the lovely child on her doorstep, surrounded by the overweening weeds of the front yard, that she simply stood and stared.

The little girl was only about so high, and she was blonde and blue-eyed and fair-skinned, all the things you might think, and she was wearing just the prettiest of neat pink pinafores and there were soft pink ribbons tied in big floppy bows in her hair and her little white socks were pulled up neatly around her ankles (and not a spot of mud on them!) and her black patent leather Mary Janes were polished so brightly that they reflected the sunshine into the witch's eyes and made them tear.

"I'm lost," the child said in a voice that quavered fair to rival the witch's own.

The witch, who was beginning now to recover her wits a little, bent closer to the child and stared sharply into her blue eyes. "Lost?" she inquired carefully, a hint of an involuntary cackle starting at the back of her throat.

The child, her lovely blue eyes wide and frightened, nodded up at the hovering witch.

"Is that right?" said the witch, just managing to choke back the monstrous cackle that threatened to erupt.

"Yes," the child murmured in a pathetic little voice, lower lip hinting at a tremble. "I'm lost and I'm hungry and I'm cold and I'm frightened." With that said—which seemed, the witch noted with pleasure, to thoroughly sap what little strength remained to her—the child lowered her head and stared, in time-honored fashion, at her patent leather shoes.

"Hmm," the witch said. "Lost, eh? And hungry and cold? And frightened? You did say frightened, didn't you? I thought you did. You did, didn't you?" She peered narrowly at the child.

The little girl nodded without looking up from her contemplation of her shoes.

Lost, the witch thought to herself, and hungry and cold and, best of all, frightened. Frightened! A silent cackle of glee shook her rounded shoulders.

"Well, then," she cried, "you must come right in, mustn't you?" and she threw the door wide open.

So eager was the witch to draw the child into the house, where she could all the better enjoy the little one's thorough-going misery, that she failed to note the disparity of truth between the child's claim of being cold and the obviously warm sunshine that had been all the while bathing her own wrinkled face in its rays.

The interior of the house, as suggested earlier, was a paragon of nastiness, with its musty gray sheets and dusty gray shelves and snapping and groaning floorboards and the cat yowling piteously in the cellar, to make no mention of the noisome brew now bubbling madly on the stove. The child seemed not to notice. Rather, she gave the appearance of a child who has suddenly found shelter from the storm, although, in this particular instance, of course, storm there was none. This important fact the witch still failed to notice, so gleeful was she at the odd twist of fate that had brought suffering and attendant misery raining down, so she thought, on the child's head.

"Lost, eh?" she cackled with delight, and rubbed her hands together. "And hungry? And cold? And frightened? You are frightened, aren't you? You said you were frightened. Would it be safe to assume you are still frightened? Maybe even just a little more frightened than before? A little? Eh? Eh?" She continued rubbing her hands vigorously together in an absolute transport of wicked pleasure. This was no mean feat, as her gnarled and bony fingers kept getting in the way of each other and threatening to tangle up beyond all hope of untangling. But rub away she did, unmindful of the danger. "Eh? Eh?"

"Oh, yes," the child dutifully replied, "much more frightened than before."

"Heh, heh," said the witch. Clearly, she still hadn't caught on about the sunlight.

After some minutes spent in very pleasant contemplation of the child's dejected look and drooping head, the witch took hold of the little girl's shoulder, being careful to press her bony but strong fingers painfully into the tender flesh, and drew the child across the room until they stood together before the stove.

"Do you see this big old pot?" the witch asked, her voice positively husky with excitement and anticipation.

"Yes'm," the child said politely.

"And can you guess what I'm cooking in that pot?"

Saying this, the witch had all she could do to keep her fingers pressed hard into the child's shoulder, so great was the urge to rub her hands together.

The child, her wide eyes barely on a level with the top of the stove and the bottom of the pot, shook her head in silence.

"No, of course not," cried the witch, barely containing her excitement, "of course you can't! You're too little to see into the pot, aren't you? Too little, too tiny, too . . . too . . ." Words failed her at this point and she had to feign a violent coughing spell to conceal the chortling that threatened to shake her old bones apart.

When at last she managed to catch her breath, the witch asked the child, as innocently as she could manage (which, as you may imagine, wasn't all that innocent but was, so the witch figured, close enough to fool a dumb little kid), "Would you like me to lift you up so you can look into the pot yourself?"

"Yes, please," the child whispered in her tiniest little voice, and bobbed her head up and down.

"Oh, boy! Oh, boy!" cried the witch, and shivered from head to toe. "I mean, oh, toys, oh, toys, yes, that's right, we must find you some toys to play with, toys, of course, oh, won't that be lovely to have some new toys!" The witch, to give credit where it's due, hadn't really made all that bad a recovery from her little slip there. But, suddenly worried that she might miss her opportunity, she instantly thought, better get on with the thing while the getting's good. Here's the child, here's the pot, pop her right in while the brew's still hot!

"Well, then," said the witch, in as close as she could get to a soothing voice, "let's get on with it, shall we?" And with that, she clasped the child around her teensy waist, squeezed as hard as she could, and lifted the child up, up, up toward the rim of the steaming, bubbling pot.

"Upsa daisy!" cried the witch as she lifted the silent child.

For a single timeless moment, witch and child hung suspended over the pot, peering—with very different thoughts and emotions, it may be assumed—through the swirling vapors to the surface of the brew.

All manner of unpleasant things floated there among the bubbles, then bobbed beneath the surface, only to be replaced by even more unpleasant things. Some of the objects had the vague shape of things you might think you recognize in a fog but that turn out to be something else. Some others appeared to be only parts of things, unknowable without the wholes from which they had been—dare we say it?—detached. Plus other things it's best not to mention at all. Considered in its entirety, it was a noxious brew and, beyond this, the less said about it the better.

The fumes swirled around the heads of the witch and the child. In that single timeless moment, neither moved, neither spoke.

And it was just at that precise moment of high drama and exquisite tension that the witch heard the "Toot, toot!" of the U.P.S fellow, a sound as hated as it was familiar.

"Oh, blast!" she snarled. "Blast and drat! Isn't that always the way! Just go and get involved in something for a minute and the whole world decides to phone you up or come knocking at the door or tooting in the road. Blast! Blast! Blast!" She actually shook with rage and frustration, clearly giving not a moment's thought to the fact that no one had phoned her up or, until the arrival of the child, come knocking at her door in absolute millennia—with the exception of the U.P.S. fellow who, of course, confined himself to tooting and never actually knocked. Some people, witches in particular, are determined to be miserable.

"Meoooooow!" cried the cat in the cellar.

Emitting a sound very like "Grrrr!" but not actually that, the witch reluctantly lowered the child to the floor.

"It's that blasted U.P.S. fellow! Careless boob! Toots his fool head off out there like a lunatic, then dumps my parcels in the mud. Leaves them out there in the hot sun to go bad, he does. Deliberate, I know it's deliberate. Does it just to get my goat!" (In point of fact, someone else had made off with her goat years before, but that's another matter entirely.) The witch uttered a few more grrrr-like noises, gave the pot a perfunctory stir, pinched the child's arm, then pinched it again for good measure, and shuffled slowly, in the approved fashion, toward the door. Halfway across the dim and dusty room, she paused and looked back at the child.

"Now, I don't want you moving, child, you hear? Not one step! Do you hear me?" She waggled a crooked finger at the little girl by way of punctuation.

"Yes'm," said the child, who looked for all the world as if she were unlikely ever to move again.

The witch grunted, squinted briefly but fiercely at the little girl, then resumed her interrupted shuffle toward the door.

Without looking back again, she angrily flung the door open. The hinges squealed in rusty protest and the door, none too sturdy to begin with and unused to such treatment, shivered and shook, as if in fright, when it slammed back hard against the wall. Muttering imprecations, as the witches' universal handbook recommends in situations such as this, the witch shuffled on out the doorway, across the broken step, and down the weedy path to the gate by the road.

Behind her, the door slammed again.

The witch, her entire attention taken up with picking her way through the tangle of weeds that threatened to trip her at every step, with muttering imprecations, and with pulling every now and again at the tuft of hairs in the tip of her chin, missed it.

Were one inclined to be flip about what was really a very serious situation for all concerned, one might say that at this point in the affair, the child was, to borrow an apt expression from the field of sport, home free.

The witch, oblivious of her predicament, reached the leaning gate at last and there in the mud at her feet lay a package, its top bearing the familiar label from her regular supplier of squiggly things.

"Ruined!" cried the witch, her voice as sharp and piercing as her fingernails, when she saw the condition of the package. "Blast that U.P.S. fellow! Blast him! Oh, blast him!" Once again, one corner of the package had burst apart, it seemed, and a number of the squiggly things it had contained, whose destiny would otherwise have brought them to the witch's stewpot, were already in the process of squiggling hurriedly away.

Moving faster than she had in centuries, the witch bent forward (she was already bent halfway forward to start with, you'll recall) and snatched at the squiggly things before they could completely effect their escape. Taking into account the witch's diminutive stature, it would be less than accurate to describe her state as a towering rage, but she was plenty angry, make no mistake about it. Gathering up as many of the little squiggly things as she could catch, she transferred them all to one hand and picked up the broken package with the other. What with the slippery texture of the things themselves, and the arthritis that stiffened the old witch's fingers, she was not having an easy time of it, and it would be as well at this point if we decline to repeat the awful things she cried out and the maledictions she promised to bring down on the head of the U.P.S. fellow.

The U.P.S. fellow, for his part, would have been shaken to his very boots, were this an ordinary occasion. But on this particular occasion, as it happens, he had concealed himself, unbeknownst to the witch, in the weeds of the yard. By stretching up on tippy-toe, he could just catch a glimpse of her struggles with the squiggly things, while yet concealing himself from her view. The sight, it may truly be reported, pleased him just no end. He was actually smiling.

When finally the witch had hold of as many of the squiggly things as she could manage, she started the long and difficult shuffle back up the path to the door. And never mind what she said on the way.

Bent double as she was, and with her mind on other matters, she only learned that the door of the house—her very own house, her oh so comfy old house, made of all her favorite things, dried cabbage leaves and stale bagels and various odds and ends of cafeteria foods, otherwise unidentified—was closed, shut tight, when the top of her head went *thunk!*, very hard, against it. She staggered back a few steps and let out a yelp of pain. In the cellar, the cat cried, "Meoooooow!" Flailing her arms to regain her balance, the witch dropped the remains of the broken package and the handful of squiggly things she'd been holding onto so carefully. The squiggly things, forewarned by their previous experience and now familiar with the terrain, lost not a moment in squiggling hastily into the weeds and out of sight, every last one of them.

The witch reeled about dizzily in the yard for a minute or two before attaining a very shaky equilibrium. When she felt a little steadier on her feet, she ventured a few tentative steps toward the door. Stunned by the unexpected turn of events, she hesitated for a moment, but then, true to form, her witchy nature prevailed and she shrieked out some perfectly dreadful things. She was a sly one, you know, and she had needed only a moment's reflection to figure out that it was the pretty little child who had closed the door of her own house on her.

"Let me in this instant!" was the gist of her cries, together with various pronouncements on the child's nature, her past, and her probable future.

There was no reply from the house.

It was at this point that the witch realized that all of her squiggly things had made good their escape. Her rage, without exaggeration, knew no bounds.

When finally her throat grew hoarse from screeching, the witch fell silent except for the wheezing of her breath. In the near-silence then, she heard a sound—two words, actually—that chilled her to the bone. The words, in a voice that quavered not at all, came from the other side of the door, her own door!

"Who's there?" said the voice, unmistakably that of the child, but changed, ominously different, transformed by the reversal of roles.

"Who's there?" the voice demanded again when the witch, momentarily startled into silence, didn't answer up quickly.

The witch would have answered up quickly enough that time, you can count on it, except that she was further surprised to find that her teeth were chattering with sudden cold, despite the otherwise warming rays of the sun. All this while, you see, all these thousands of years, it had been the steam from the bubbling stewpot, with its hideous gumbo of squiggly things, that had given her the only warmth she had ever known. Now, deprived of her stewpot—and even of her fresh supply of squiggly things, for the matter of that—she suddenly felt the cold pinching at her with fingers as merciless as her own.

"Who's there?" the child's voice, positively stertorous by this juncture, demanded yet again.

"Me," the witch only just managed to whimper.

"Never heard of you!" snapped the voice of the child. "Go away! Beat it! Scram!"

Then there came a sound from the other side of the door that sent the worst shudder yet through the shivering body of the old witch. It was the sound of a heavy iron bar being slammed into place against the door. The dramatic effect of the sound was considerably enhanced by the fact that never, until now, had the door had such a bar to shut it so effectively. It was, all in all, a sound that the witch would have described as very—had she been more articulate just at the moment—*final*.

"Oh, my gosh!" said the witch.

"Meooooow!" said the cat.

"Heh, heh!" said the child.

"Toot, toot!" said the U.P.S. fellow.

Puddle

ARTHUR PORGES

A great poet promised to show us fear in a handful of dust. If ever I doubted that such a thing were possible, I know better now. In the past few weeks a vague, terrible memory of my childhood suddenly came into sharp focus after staying tantalizingly just beyond the edge of recall for decades. Perhaps the high fever from a recent virus attack opened some blocked pathways in my brain, but whatever the explanation, I have come to understand for the first time why I see fear not in dust, but in water.

It must seem quite absurd: fear in a shallow puddle made by rain; but think about it for a moment. Haven't you ever, as a child, gazed down at such a little pool on the street, seen the reflected sky, and experienced the illusion, very strongly, so that it brought a shudder, of endless depth a mere step away—a chasm extending downward some-how to the heavens? A single stride to the center of the glassy puddle, and you would fall right through. Down? Up? The direction was indefinable, a weird blend of both. There were clouds beneath your feet, and nothing but that shining surface between. Did you dare to take that critical step and shatter the illusion? Not I. Now that memory has returned, I recall being far too scared of the consequences. I carefully skirted such wet patches, no matter how casu-ally my friends splashed through.

Most of my acquaintances tolerated this weakness in me. After all, I held my own in most of the games we played. It was only after Joe Carma appeared in town that my own little hell materialized, and I lost status.

He was three years older than I, and much stronger; thickset, muscular, dark—and perpetually surly. He was never known to smile in any joyous way, but only to laugh with a kind of *schadenfreude*, the German word for mirth provoked by another's misfortunes. Few could stand up to him when he hunched his blocky frame and bored in with big fists flailing, and I wasn't one of the elect; he terrified me as much by his demeanor as by his physical power.

Looking back now, I discern something grim and evil about the boy, fatherless, with a weak and querulous moth-er. What he did was not the thoughtless, basically merry mischief of the other kids, but full of malice and cruelty. Where Shorty Dugan would cheerfully snowball a tomcat, or let the air out of old man Gruber's tires, Carma pre-ferred to torture a kitten—rumor said he'd been seen burn-ing one alive—or take a hammer to a car's headlights.

Somehow Joe Carma learned of my phobia about puddles, and my torment began. On several occasions he meant to go so far as to collar me, hold my writhing body over one of the bigger pools, and pretend to drop me through—into that terribly distant sky beyond the sidewalk.

Each time I was saved at the last moment, nearly hysterical with fright, by Larry Dumont, who was taller than the bully, at least as strong, and more agile. They were bound to clash eventually, but so far Carma had sheered off, hoping, perhaps, to find and exploit some weakness in his opponent that would give him an edge. Not that he was a coward, just coldly careful; one who always played the odds.

As for Larry, he was good-natured, and not likely to fight at all unless pushed into it. By grabbing Carma with his lean, wiry fingers that could bend thick nails, and half-jokingly arguing with him, Dumont would bring about my release without forcing a showdown. Then they might scuffle a bit, with Larry smiling and Joe darkly sullen as ever, only to separate, newly respectful of each other's strength.

One day, after a heavy rain, Carma caught me near a giant puddle—almost a pond—that had appeared behind the Johnson barn at the north end of town. It was a lonely spot, the hour was rather early, and ordinarily Joe would not have been about, as he liked to sleep late on weekends. If I had suspected he might be around, that was the last place in the world I'd have picked to visit alone.

Fear and fascination often go together. I stood by the huge puddle, but well away from the edge, peering down at the blue sky, quite cloudless and so far beneath the ground where it should not have been at all; and for the thousandth time tried to gather enough nerve to step in. I *knew* there had to be solid land below—jabs with a stick had proved this much before in similar cases—yet I simply could not make my feet move.

At that instant brawny arms seized me, lifted my body into the air, and tilted it so that my contorted face was parallel to the pool and right over the glittering surface.

"Gonna count to ten, and then drop you right through!" a rasping voice taunted me. "You been right all along: it's a long way down. You're gonna fall and fall, with the wind whistling past your ears; turning, tumbling, faster and faster. You'll be gone for good, kid, just sailing down forever. You're gonna scream like crazy all the way, and it'll get fainter and fainter. Here we go: one! two! three!—"

I tried to scream but my throat was sealed. I just made husky noises while squirming desperately, but Carma held me fast. I could feel the heavy muscles in his arms all knotted with the effort.

"—four! five! Won't be long now. Six! seven!—"

A thin, whimpering sound broke from my lips, and he laughed. My vision was blurring; I was going into shock, it seems to me now, years later.

Then help came, swift and effective. Carma was jerked back, away from the water, and I fell free. Larry Dumont stood there, white with fury.

"You're a dirty skunk, Joe!" he growled angrily. "You need a lesson, your own kind."

Then he did an amazing thing. Although Carma was heavier than he, if shorter, Larry whipped those lean arms around the bully, snatched him clear of the ground, and with a single magnificent heave threw him fully six feet into the middle of the water.

Now I wonder about my memory; I have to. Did I actually see what I now recall so clearly? It's quite impossible, but the vision persists. Carma fell full-length, face down, in the puddle, and surely the water could not have been more than a few inches deep. But he went on through! I saw his body twisting, turning, and shrinking in size as it dropped away into that cloudless sky. He screamed, and it was exactly as he had described it to me moments earlier. The terrible, shrill cries grew fainter, as if dying away in the distance; the flailing figure became first a tiny doll, and then a mere dot; an unforgettable thing, surely, yet only a dream-memory for so long.

I looked at Larry; he was gaping, his face drained of all blood. His long fingers were still hooked and tense from that mighty toss.

That's how I remember it. Perhaps we probed the puddle; I'm not sure, but if we did, surely it was inches deep.

On recovering from my illness three weeks ago, I hired a good private detective to make a check. The files of the local paper are unfortunately not complete, but one item for August 20, 1937, when I was eight, begins:

NO CLUES ON DISAPPEARANCE
OF CARMA BOY

After ten days of police investigation, no trace has been found of Joe Carma, who vanished completely on the ninth of this month. It is not even known how he left town, if he did, since there is no evidence that he went by either bus or train. Martin's Pond, the only deep water within many miles, was dragged, but without any result.

The detective assures me that Joe Carma never returned to town, and that the name is unlisted in army records, with the FBI, or indeed any national roster from 1937 to date.

These days, I skin-dive, sail my own little sloop, and have even shot some of the worst Colorado River rapids in a rubber boat. Yet it still takes almost more courage than I have to slosh through a shallow puddle that mirrors the sky.

Witch and Cousin

MAGGIE WAGNER-HANKINS

My cousin Alice claimed to be a witch. I'd never met her till my mother and I traveled south into Arkansas for my Grandmother Herrington's funeral last summer. This was my father's mother, and Mom and I hadn't kept in touch with that side of the family since the divorce, but Mom decided I ought to attend my grandmother's funeral.

Maybe she felt it would help make up for the fact that my father was out of the country and couldn't get back in time for the services. She came along as chauffeur, since I was only sixteen at the time and she didn't want me driving long distances by myself. She probably also figured it was a good way to get a few days off work without anyone's getting upset. Who could say no to a request to attend your mother-in-law's funeral?

I thought my cousin Alice would be happier to see me. All she said when we were introduced was, "So you're Celia. Well, we meet at last." She wasn't exactly rude, but she had this cold, distant attitude that made me feel even more a stranger than I was.

She steered clear of me that first day we were there, and all through the funeral the next morning, but after it was over I looked up from the rock where I was sitting, out at the edge of her yard, just thinking about things, and there she was.

"Nice of you to show up now," she said, flinging her long, almost white hair back over her shoulder. "Where were you the last two years when Granny was so sick?"

As if I could help it that I hadn't been here! And how would I have known our grandmother was sick? I tried explaining this to her, but she just shrugged.

"It doesn't matter," she said. "You're here now. Soon you'll be gone, and then I won't be bothered with you again."

"You don't have to be 'bothered' with me now," I said, already tired of her tone of voice. "You came over here to *me*, remember?"

"So I did. Let's be friends, Celia. It'll make things easier. We need to talk."

I wondered if her abrupt manner was typical of all Arkansans or if it was only a personal trait of hers, like her tendency not to look me in the eye when she spoke.

"Okay," I said cautiously. "Fine. I'd hoped we could be friends."

She just smiled, her eyes turning suddenly sly, and said, "Let's find someplace a little more private to talk. You'll be leaving in an hour, and we hardly even know each other."

And whose fault is that? I wanted to say. I've been here since yesterday morning. Instead I got up and trailed her into the house, a dutiful guest following orders.

Her room looked like something from a horror movie—black, red, and dark, thanks to the black window shades. Instead of turning on a light, she plopped down on the red carpet by her bed, motioning for me to do the same.

"My mom would kill me if my room looked like this," I said.

"Oh, my folks are used to it. They've given up on me." It was then that she broke the big news. "Did you know I'm a witch?" she asked casually.

I laughed, figuring she would, too. She didn't.

"I *am*. Granny was, too. You know that, cousin? You're Granny's granddaughter the same as me, so you might even be part witch yourself."

"Oh? Is that a fact?" I asked, wondering where this was leading. I decided to go along with her game. "But why only part? Maybe I'm a full-fledged witch."

"Oh no. You're only part witch. Actually, so am I, for the time being."

"Well, Alice, I'll tell you what. You can be the full-time witch for our family. I have other things to keep myself occupied."

"That's kind of what I had in mind," she said, studying her long nails. "Did you know, Celia, that our birthdays are exactly six months apart? Yours is May third and mine is November third. That makes us opposites on the zodiac wheel—Taurus and Scorpio. We were born the same year, too."

"Interesting."

"Isn't it?" She met my eye just briefly out of the corner of hers.

"Is all this leading somewhere?" I asked.

"As a matter of fact, it is," she said. "I need something from you."

"From me? What?"

"Your power."

That one caught me by surprise. I laughed again. "My power? You want to go into a little more detail on that?"

"We're not just cousins," she said. "We're actually—two parts of a whole. We're almost exact complements."

"Oh? In what way?" I had to admit she was good at building suspense. "Besides being—how did you put that?—'opposites on the zodiac wheel'?"

"Well, look at yourself," said Alice. "Your hair is almost black. Mine is almost white. What hand do you write with?"

"My left."

"I'm right-handed."

"Most people are."

"Then why aren't you?" she asked. I had no answer.

"What's your best subject in school? No, wait! Let me guess. English. And you were a spelling bee champ in grade school, right?"

I was amazed. "But how did you—"

"Lucky guess, cousin. *My* best subject is math. And I won the science fair in fifth grade. I'm terrible in English, and I can't spell to save my soul. My guess is that you've always had a little trouble with math."

She was right. Somewhere a door closed, but I barely

noticed. Witch or not, Alice had me hooked. I'd heard that the best storytellers are from the South. I was beginning to believe it.

"Even our names—" she said. "Alice, Celia. Same letters, all mixed around." She waited for that to sink in, then continued, "What else? I hate vegetables. You?"

I thought about lying to her, but I knew she could find it out easily enough by asking my mother, which I didn't put past her. I admitted sheepishly, "I'm—a vegetarian."

She gave a hoot of a laugh and slapped her leg. "I knew it! So, you believe me now? Two parts of a whole?"

"It's an interesting theory," I admitted. "Except that I don't believe anyone is only part of a person. Where did you hear all this, anyway? From our grandmother?"

"Actually, yes. Granny was part of a whole with a cousin of hers. They were born six months apart, same as us. And guess what? They died exactly six months apart, too."

There was a knock at the door. "Celia, are you in there?" It was my mother.

"We're just chatting," Alice called out. "Can we have another fifteen minutes or so?"

"Sure," said Mom, probably thrilled that we were finally speaking to each other. "Have fun."

"So, all this has been really interesting," I told Alice, "but let's get back to that other thing you were talking about. About wanting my power. What does that mean?"

"It means, dear cousin, that we're both witches—or *part* witches—because that runs in families. Now, we could *share* our powers, the way Granny and her cousin did. They always did their spells together."

"What kind of spells?" I asked cautiously. I still could hardly believe this whole thing wasn't a joke cooked up by Alice, to try to fool her "city slicker" cousin. But if it wasn't a joke, then she was obviously a little crazy, and there was no sense in making her mad.

"All kinds. Matchmaking, healing—"

"Could you make people do things against their will?" I asked. "You know, bewitch them?"

"They could have. Granny said they had when they were younger, but later they concentrated on helping people with their powers. Personally, I'd say that was a waste. Let people take care of their own problems."

"Well, what would *you* use the power for, then?" I asked.

"To get ahead in the world, like any normal person." She acted as if I'd asked the stupidest question in the world. "I may not have been born with money, but I'll have all I need, and everything else I want, too—perfect job if I feel like working, best-looking guys, great homes all over— once I have the power."

"And why would I want to give you any power?" I asked. "If I could, that is."

"Because, cousin, I have a feeling your half has already been more of a burden to you than you've cared for. Am I right?"

"I don't know what you're talking about," I said, feeling a little twinge in the pit of my stomach.

"Don't you?" she asked, for once looking me straight in the eye. This time I was the one to look away. "You mean you've never felt something working in you—working *through* you—that you couldn't explain?"

I thought a minute. Should I admit to the few times I'd known ahead of time that something was going to happen, or the way the plants in my house seemed to perk up before my very eyes when I sent them loving thoughts and gently stroked their leaves? Or the way I'd look at certain strangers and know their problems, and feel so powerless to help?

"No," I said. "I've never felt anything like that."

She just looked at me for a minute, then slowly moved her face closer to mine. Her eyes were ice blue, even in the near-dark. "Either you're lying," she said quietly, "or you're stupid. Let me give you some examples from my life, and maybe you'll 'remember' something."

I nodded.

"Okay. I have precognition sometimes. I know when something is going to happen, and it always does, just the way I see it. Sound familiar?"

"No," I lied.

"Once I made a dog jump in a pond in the middle of winter, just by using my mind power on him," she said. "And I made Miranda Payson, the smartest girl in my class, write the wrong answers on a test and get an F. It was the first one she ever got. Boy, was she shocked."

She sat back against the bed and laughed quietly.

"I wouldn't think those things would be something to be proud of, even if you *did* do them, which I doubt."

"Oh, I did them, all right. And I was *very* proud of it. It was hard work. But it was worth it because it proved I did have some of the power."

"Sounds like you have enough power as it is," I said. "Any more and you could be dangerous."

"Oh, that was just kid stuff," said Alice. "I won't be wasting my time on things like that. There are bigger fish in the sea. And don't start feeling sorry for the world. I won't mess with anyone who doesn't mess with me first."

We sat quietly for a few seconds, then she turned and said, "So what about it, cousin? Feel like handing over the reins? Don't worry, I'd make it worth your while. I never forget a favor. And aren't you about ready to stop having those nightmares?"

Nightmares? So she knew about those, too. But how? Was she having the same dreams?

"You've had them, too, haven't you?" she said. "Running through the woods just at twilight, desperately following someone, chasing a wisp of dark hair, feeling panicky without knowing why. Except in *your* dream you're probably running down city streets, chasing a wisp of *white* hair."

I didn't want to, but I nodded.

"That's *me* you're chasing," she explained. "Your other half. And you almost find me, except when you suddenly come to a lake you realize you're too late. The white hair— *my* hair—is disappearing beneath the surface. And you know you have to come in, too, because you're the other part. Against your will, you step into the water. It's so cold. You start to sink down into—"

"Stop it!" I said sharply. "Just shut up."

"I thought so." Her voice was smug.

I took a few deep breaths. "So you think it's possible for me to—*give* you—what you're calling my 'power'?"

"Oh, I know it is. Granny told me. She knew about you

and me. She knew more about you than you might think. She had her ways of keeping up with people, and you *were* special to her, even if you never heard from her. So how 'bout it? Your mom'll be back any minute."

"Fine." I jumped up, suddenly tired of the whole thing. It had to be a joke, or some delusion my nutty cousin was having. So we'd just play it out to its end, and then I could forget about it and forget about her. We'd be back in Kansas City in ten hours, and I could get on with my life.

"Great. Step over here," she said, leading me to a massive dark wood desk. "This was Granny's desk." On it were two small bowls, one silver-colored and one gold. Beside the gold-colored bowl was a white candle in a gold candle holder, and to the left of the silver bowl was a black candle in a silver holder. In the center was a small black box.

Alice seemed a little nervous, and I could tell she was trying to hurry. She knew this wouldn't be the perfect time for my mother to pop her head into the room.

"Now let me explain what's going to happen," she said, lighting the candles. "We'll each pull three of our hairs out and place them in our bowl. Also, an eyelash and a little piece of fingernail. You have the gold bowl, I'll take the silver. Then we burn the stuff in the bowl. I take some of the ash out of each bowl and smear a circle on your forehead. When I draw my hand away, I've taken your power, and you're free."

Free. Free of the nightmares, I thought. And free of knowing things before they happen. I've never been crazy about that. I wonder if it will affect my plants.

"Let's do it," she said, handing me a book of matches.

I barely felt the sharp pain as I yanked my hair out. It wasn't long before we both had what we needed in the bowls. We each set a lighted match to the contents, and watched as our hair fried in an instant. The fingernail took a little longer. Finally, she was satisfied that we had enough ash.

"Okay, cousin," she said, rubbing her index finger in first her bowl, then mine. "I won't forget this. When I'm at the top of the heap, I'll send for you."

A funny feeling came over me as she touched me. "That won't be necessary," I said. When she had rubbed a circle on my forehead, she pulled her finger away. I have to say I was tingling.

"Now!" she said with a triumphant smile. "In this box is a message from Granny. She said if you ever did decide to give me your half of the power, we should open this box and read the message. I've been so tempted to peek at it, but I figured it might ruin the spell or something." She picked up the box with trembling fingers.

"Feeling all right?" I asked, the strange, glowing feeling still hanging over me.

"Not really," she said. "This whole thing has wiped me out. After you leave, I'm going to take a long nap."

"That's a good idea, cousin," I said quietly.

She opened the box and pulled out a folded piece of paper. Unfolding it, she held it close to a candle, squinting to read it. "I can't—seem to make this out. It's all— scribbly or something—"

"Let me see it," I said, feeling curiously at ease. I took the paper out of her hand. Though the figures were unfamiliar to me, I had no trouble reading them.

I smiled. "Oh dear," I said, barely concealing my grin.

"What?" She looked panicky. "Stop playing games and give me back the paper." She tried to snatch it from me but, somehow, her hand missed it.

"What for? You can't read it anyway," I said, my voice still calm. "But I can. Shall I tell you what Grandmother Herrington has to say?"

"You can't read it either."

"Guess again—*cousin*. Here goes. 'So you've tried it, have you, Alice dear? I wish I hadn't had to be less than truthful with you, but after years of watching you grow more selfish and self-centered, with never a care for anyone but yourself, I knew I couldn't possibly lead you to a greater power. I knew you'd be better off without even the part you had, so I'm glad you've gotten to this point. Celia, I've been very aware of you, too, even though you've only seen me a time or two in your dreams. You're a good, loving, caring person, and I know that this power can be trusted to you for the right use. Don't let it be a burden. It doesn't have to be. But when you need a little help in your work as a healer of the planet, which you're already showing signs of being, don't be frightened of it, either. Now, Alice, don't even think about trying to get even with your cousin. You can't hurt her, and she won't hurt you, so why not try to part on good terms. I love you both, always, Granny Herrington.' "

Alice just stood there. In the candlelight her face looked like a grotesque mask, eyes wide, mouth agape. I felt kind of sorry for her. Now that we were, in a way, bound together more closely than I'd have guessed possible, I felt all her pain and frustration as intensely as if they'd been my own. Except I knew they were her feelings and not mine.

A knock at the door made Alice jump.

It was Mom again. "Celia, we really do need to take off, honey."

"Coming," I called out, folding the paper and tucking it into my skirt pocket. "Alice and I are just saying our good-byes."

I took Alice's hand, a gesture that made her wince but one she seemed powerless to prevent. "I'm sorry you won't have any help making it to the top. But I have the feeling that, if you really want to wind up there, you'll find another way. Still, I wish you'd think it over. They say it's lonely at the top."

She hated me. It was clear as crystal from the look in her eyes. She didn't say a word as I squeezed her hand and said, "You let me know if you need anything. Your parents have our number. I mean it. You were right. We really are two parts of a whole."

I had the sudden feeling that my grandmother was there in the room with us. I could even see her face— smiling, now. It was a face I'd seen in my dreams but had never recognized.

"At least now *you* won't have the nightmares any-more," I told Alice. "If you do have that dream again, you'll dream that it's me who's chased you to the lake, but when you jump in, you won't be there for long, because I'll be grabbing you by those wisps of white hair and pulling you right back out again."

"Don't do me any favors," she said softly. Then she

stalked to the door, jerked it open, and waited for me to leave. An almost blinding shaft of light entered the room from the hallway. As I walked past her, I wanted more than anything to ease her pain. But this time, when I reached out to her, she avoided my touch. I heard the door slam shut behind me.

It didn't matter. I was the one with the power now. And she could try all she wanted, but she wouldn't stop me from caring about her, or checking in on her from time to time. Like it or not, I was going to do my best to help her get her act together.

And someday, after she managed to find the decent human being she'd buried somewhere inside herself, maybe I'd even give her back some of the power. I could do that. She didn't know it, but I did, thanks to the P.S. at the end of our grandmother's letter, which I knew had been meant for my eyes only.

I Can't
Help Saying
Goodbye

ANN MACKENZIE

My name is Karen Anders I'm nine years old I'm little and dark and nearsighted I live with Max and Libby I have no friends

Max is my brother he's twenty years older than me he has close-together eyes and a worried look we Anders always were a homely lot he has asthma too

Libby used to be pretty but she's put on weight she looks like a wrestler in her new bikini I wish I had a bikini Lib won't buy me one I guess I'd stop being so scared of going in the water if I had a yellow bikini to wear on the beach

Once when I was seven my father and mother went shopping they never came home there was a holdup at the bank like on television Lib said this crazy guy just mowed them down

Before they went out I knew I had to say goodbye I said it slow and clear goodbye Mommy first then goodbye Daddy but no one took any notice of it much seeing they were going shopping anyway but afterwards Max remembered he said to Libby the way that kid said goodbye you'd think she knew

Libby said for gosh sakes how could she know be reasonable honey but I guess this means we're responsible for her now have you thought of that

She didn't sound exactly pleased about it

Well after I came to live with Max and Libby I knew I had to say goodbye to Lib's brother Dick he was playing cards with them in the living room and when Lib yelled Karen get to bed can't you I went to him and stood as straight as I could with my hands clasped loose in front like Miss Jones tells us to when we have choir in school

I said very slow and clear well goodbye Dick and Libby gave me a kind of funny look

Dick didn't look up from his cards he said goodnight kid

Next evening before any of us saw him again he was dead of a disease called peritonitis it explodes in your stomach and busts it full of holes

Lib said Max did you hear how she said goodbye to Dick and Max started wheezing and gasping and carrying on he said I told you there was something didn't I it's weird that's what it is it scares me sick who'll she say goodbye to next I'd like to know and Lib said there honey there baby try to calm yourself

I came out from behind the door where I was listening I said don't worry Max you'll be okay

His face was blotchy and his mouth was blue he said in a scratchy whisper how do you know

What a dumb question as though I'd tell him even if I did know

Libby bent down and pushed her face close to mine I could smell her breath cigarettes and bourbon and garlic salad

She said only it came out like a hiss don't you ever say goodbye to anyone again don't you ever say it

The trouble is I can't help saying goodbye

After that things went okay for a while and I thought maybe they'd forgotten all about it but Libby still wouldn't buy me a new bikini

Then one day in school I knew I had to say goodbye to Kimberley and Charlene and Brett and Susie

Well I clasped my hands in front of me and I said it to each of them slow and careful one by one

Miss Jones said goodness Karen why so solemn dear and I said well you see they're going to die

She said Karen you're a cruel wicked child you shouldn't say things like that it isn't funny see how you made poor little Susie cry and she said come Susie dear get in the car you'll soon be home and then you'll be all right

So Susie dried her tears and ran after Kimberley and Charlene and Brett and climbed in the car right next to Charlene's mom because Charlene's mom was doing the car pool that week

And that was the last we saw of any of them because the car skidded off the road to Mountain Heights and rolled all the way down to the valley before it caught fire

There was no school next day it was the funeral we sang songs and scattered flowers on the graves

Nobody wanted to stand next to me

When it was over Miss Jones came along to see Libby I said good evening and she said it back but her eyes slipped away from me and she breathed kind of fast then Libby sent me out to play

Well when Miss Jones had gone Libby called me back she said didn't I tell you never never never to say goodbye to anyone again

She grabbed hold of me and her eyes were kind of burning she twisted my arm it hurt I screamed don't please don't but she went on twisting and twisting so I said if you don't let go I'll say goodbye to Max

It was the only way I could think of to make her stop

She did stop but she kept hanging on to my arm she said oh god you mean you can make it happen you can make them die

Well of course I can't but I wasn't going to tell her that in case she hurt me again so I said yes I can

She let go of me I fell hard on my back she said are you okay did I hurt you Karen honey I said yes and you better not do it again and she said I was only kidding I didn't mean it

So then I knew that she was scared of me I said I want a bikini to wear on the beach a yellow one because yellow's my favorite color

She said well honey you know we have to be careful and I said do you want me to say goodbye to Max or not

She leaned against the wall and closed her eyes and

stood quite still for a while and I said what are you doing and she said thinking

Then all of a sudden she opened her eyes and grinned she said hey I know we'll go to the beach tomorrow we'll take our lunch I said does that mean I get my new bikini and she said yes your bikini and anything else you want

So yesterday afternoon we bought the bikini and early this morning Lib went into the kitchen and fixed up the picnic fried chicken and orange salad and chocolate cake and the special doughnuts she makes for company she said Karen are you sure it's all the way you want it and I said sure everything looks just great and I won't be so scared of the waves now I have my bikini and Libby laughed she put the lunch basket into the car she has strong brown arms she said no I guess you won't

Then I went up to my room and put on my bikini it fitted just right I went to look in the glass I looked and looked then I clasped my hands in front I felt kind of funny I said slow and clear goodbye Karen goodbye Karen goodbye goodbye

Fun and Games at the Whacks Museum

ELLIOTT CAPON

He had two windows, one on each side of the main entrance door. Both were draped in black and purple fabrics. In the window to your left was a life-sized likeness of President Kennedy, waving and smiling and looking like he did right before he was shot. The workmanship was so extraordinary and the tragedy so recent that ninety-nine out of a hundred people who walked past the window would swear that the president was standing there, breathing and looking you right in the eye. In the other window was a fantasy creation, a person sort of split into two people, like Siamese twins. One half was an astonishingly lifelike representation of Anthony Perkins holding an ax, and he sort of melded into the other side of the figure, which looked like Anthony Perkins dressed as his mother, and she was wielding a large knife. It was because of this statue with its deadly cutlery that me and Pat Carter and Vince Riposo and all the other kids referred to the place as Berrigan's "Whacks" Museum.

All this took place in the town of Bellerive, which was French for Pretty River, though of course the French had sold the place to John Adams or Andrew Jackson long before the rubber processing plant turned the river into a thick syrupy mess. Bellerive wasn't a particularly small town—we had a population of around twelve thousand—but it was the kind of place where everybody kinda sorta knew each other. We had four Protestant churches, a Catholic church, an A.M.E. church, even a reform synagogue. We had a VFW, a Knights of Columbus, an American Legion, an Elks Lodge, volunteer first aid squads at each end of town, and any number of PTAs. Everybody belonged to something or other, and everybody, if not known by everybody else, was at least known by *somebody* else. Several years later, I read a book called *Siege* by Edwin Corley, and one line has stuck with me for almost thirty years now: "He was aware of being black, just as Les Clayton was aware of being a redhead; so far it had not meant much more than that." That pretty much describes Bellerive. My father was chairman of the Brotherhood at the synagogue, and my best friend, Pat Carter, was black, and my other best friend, Vince, went to Catholic school. But the differences didn't mean anything. There *were* no differences. To describe Bellerive as One Big Happy Family would be to sugarcoat the truth, but there was a great sense of community, of "Belleriveness," if you will.

That, I think, was one of the reasons a lot of important people did not like Mr. Berrigan.

Berrigan's Wax—or, if you were less than fifteen years of age, the Whacks—Museum might have been swallowed up in, say, New York or Los Angeles or Chicago, but in Bellerive it was quite a magnet. We had a halfway decent state park nearby, no great shakes in and of itself but coupled with a trip to Berrigan's, a day at the park made it worth packing the family in the car and driving for an hour or so to Bellerive. So especially on weekends, and during the summer, a lot of cars would come into town, people would visit Berrigan's, and then they'd hop back in their cars for the quick ride to the park. They came from within a fifty or sixty mile radius, from towns much like Bellerive, just to see the Whacks Museum; no one came out of Berrigan's and then unloaded major shopping dollars on Frémont Street, the main shopping drag, because there was nothing on Frémont that wasn't on *their* Main Streets. The mayor, the municipal judge, the members of the Town Council—all basically decent people, I must point out—they owned a lot of the stores and businesses that adjoined Berrigan's, and you'd see them looking out their windows or biting their lips or making disgusted faces as all these people would come, pay their dollar to get into Berrigan's, and then zoom out of Bellerive without stopping off at any of the other shops along Frémont. Biggy Piggy's Family Restaurant did a little ex-Berrigan business, but most of the tourists had either packed picnic lunches or got something at the concession stand at the state park. Not that the Whacks Museum was hurting anybody, mind you, but the powers that be were resentful. That was part of it.

The second part was that Mr. Berrigan didn't belong to anything. No one knew much about him, not even us kids. He lived alone, atop the museum, and we never knew if he was a life-long bachelor, a widower, or divorced. He didn't belong to the VFW or the Elks, would come into church (sometimes the Methodist and sometimes the Baptist) usually only on Christmas Eve, and just generally did not participate in the spirit of Belleriveness that we all held so important. He never went to Town Council meetings and never attended the volunteer fire department picnic fund-raisers. Parents would drop an occasional odd remark that us kids'd pick up, and we got the impression that most of the grown-ups considered him an "odd fellow" or a "queer duck."

The third thing that, we gathered, the adults did not like about Mr. Berrigan was the rear room of the Whacks Museum, the one where us kids practically lived, me and Pat and Vince and all the other kids.

No one could then, or could now, deny that Mr. Berrigan was a genius at creating lifelike wax figures. He had an Elvis Presley and a John Wayne and Marilyn Monroe (with that dress blowing up) and a Superman and old Mahatma Gandhi and Jane Russell, you name them, they were there. His statues were remarkably, astonishingly lifelike. I think Vincent Price did about a dozen movies where the wax sculptor pours wax over living people and puts them on display, but Mr. Berrigan's statues were even better than that. The man was a superlative artist; and a dozen times a day someone would inadvertently catch himself saying "Excuse me" to, or asking a question of, one of the statues.

That was great for the old people and the tourists, but us kids always plunked down our dollar and ran right for the rear display room, the one you had to pass through the black curtain to get to, the one with the sign that read CHAMBER OF HORRORS.

He had Frankenstein and Dracula and the Wolfman and the Mummy. He had an empty pedestal with a plaque that said "The Invisible Man." He had the Creature from the Black Lagoon and Jack the Ripper and one of the Its: either "It, the Terror from Beyond Space" or "It Came from Outer Space," I could never tell them apart. He had what were claimed to be authentic torture devices from the Spanish Inquisition on which realistic victims screamed and stared at us in agony and hopelessness. He had giant spiders and bats and rats and owls whose glass eyes glittered in the indirect and dim light. It was spooky in that room and it was unnerving and it was sometimes, when your imagination got to running away with you, downright frightening. We loved it. The place was rarely without two or three or ten kids, screaming in delighted fright and joking and chasing each other with pretend claws extended. There was always the one with the morbid sense of curiosity who would stand for hours staring at the torture scenes. One of those, a kid I knew only peripherally, named Larry, would, sixteen years later, murder his parents and his in-laws and his wife and his sister-in-law, but I think that was just coincidence.

Kids at that age, roughly ten to fourteen, all go through

the horror/SF phase. We all collected and traded comic books and *Famous Monsters of Filmland* magazine and saw the latest Japanese monster movie every Saturday afternoon at the Bristol. And nobody thought much about it.

But then people, probably important people, started whispering things, things about how the back room of Berrigan's had items that were too unnerving for young, impressionable minds to be exposed to. The whisper probably started with the mayor and the other business people along Frémont, who passed it on to their wives, who brought it up at PTA meetings, where it got to all our parents, and then to us. They couldn't shut Berrigan's down, they couldn't prevent him from portraying movie monsters in his museum (they did shut down the dirty book store in less than two weeks), but they could prevent us kids from going in, from enriching Mr. Berrigan by thirty kids times a dollar a day two or three days a week. Our parents just simply refused to give us a dollar to get into the Whacks Museum, and the only way me or Pat or Vince could get in would be to save our total allowance for four weeks. And what, do without new comics or Heinlein paperbacks for a whole month just to see the same statues again? Sure, we loved the back room at Berrigan's, but we weren't willing to make that kind of sacrifice.

I don't know that Mr. Berrigan was being edged close to bankruptcy by the loss of revenue, but he must've been hurting, because most if not all of his midweek cash came from us kids. It didn't take a genius to figure out what was the cause of his sudden decline in attendance. A few weeks after the ban went into effect, Mr. Berrigan took that statue of President Kennedy out of his window and replaced it with one of Mr. Hubert, the mayor. Mr. Hubert was somewhat overweight, and tended to perspire heavily. He also had a very heavy five o'clock shadow, usually by noon. The statue Mr. Berrigan put in the window was so true to life it was uncanny. Except that the statue was a *little* more overweight than Mr. Hubert, and there were big drops of perspiration so cleverly crafted they were astonishing, and the beard stubble was just ever so slightly more pronounced than on the original model. I think if someone had signed the name "Michelangelo" on the figure, it could have stood proudly in any museum in the world.

He also turned the Norman/Mrs. Bates statue around in the other window so that it was *looking* at Mr. Hubert.

Everyone thought it was a very funny joke, everyone except the mayor, of course. But there was nothing he could do about it. Mr. Berrigan even took an ad in the *Courier*, the daily paper that covered the entire county, announcing the new display as a tribute to our fine and respected mayor.

About a week later, Pat and me (Vince wasn't there because Catholic schools were open that week, the week before Easter; he'd be off next week, when me and Pat were both back in the hell known as sixth grade) were lounging in Boston Alley, a narrow street that ran behind and parallel to Frémont. The backs of the businesses on Frémont and those of First Street were all there was on Boston Alley; it was nothing but service entrances and garbage cans. We liked to sit there because no one ever came down it and we could pretend anything we wanted to.

This day we were playing FBI, looking for a Commie spy who had made off with the plans for the secret moon rocket and had eluded us by ducking down this alley. We were trying all the doors to see if he had entered one of the buildings. (He was going to have entered the Printrite Shop, where we were going to chase him into a vat of sophomoric acid and chalk up another victory for J. Edgar Hoover.) Pat turned the doorknob on the service entrance to the Whacks Museum . . . it turned. He pushed the door open and he looked at me. We must've looked like mirror images of each other: eyes and mouths wide open, torn between curiosity and flight. Pat decided it.

"Let's go in," he whispered.

It being a school holiday, we knew that there would be a trickling of tourists in the place, keeping Mr. Berrigan busy. So we went in. We were on a small landing, with a few steps leading up to a door we knew led to the Chamber of Horrors, and a longer flight of stairs leading downward. Mr. Berrigan knew us, of course, and if he saw us in the museum he'd know we hadn't paid to get in, so we both naturally headed down the stairs. I carefully closed the door behind us, making sure it didn't snap lock.

The staircase took a turn, and as we rounded it both of us gasped. We were in the basement of the Whacks Museum, and it looked like the dream mad scientist's laboratory.

There was a giant vat of what I assumed and still assume was wax, or paraffin, or whatever the figures were made of, heated with steam coils and gently simmering. There was a table the size of the USS *Lexington* with the tools of

Mr. Berrigan's trade: knives and scrapers and spatulas and wires and glass eyes and wigs. But more important, more impressive, more absolutely, incredibly, sixth-grade *wonderful* were the works in progress. All over the room there rested heads, arms and legs, and torsos. A half-finished President Johnson head sat on a table; there was a headless and armless body that was dressed in cowboy clothes— Marshall Dillon, I presume? Or maybe Bat Masterson? Hideous monster faces stood on wire bodies or hung from hooks on the wall, including one that would, some twenty years later, bear a striking resemblance to one E.T. I picked up a fully-formed scaly arm from the table and growled, thrusting it at Pat; he responded by holding an alien's head up in front of his own and lunging at me. We laughed, but then quickly strangled the noise. We just wanted to look, and we certainly didn't want to get caught. We examined, explored, gaped, and exclaimed for about a half hour, until we heard a creaking that frightened us. We bolted up the stairs and back out into Boston Alley, congratulating ourselves on our feat of bravery and derring-do, the Commie spy having blithely made his way back to Moscow with the secret plan.

That Saturday we took Vince with us, and the three of us crept back down to the workroom. The cowboy turned out to be an astonishing likeness of Nick Adams, "The Rebel." Again, we stayed for a few minutes, touching but not removing anything, and skulked out.

We discovered that the door was never locked, at least not during the day, and Pat and I, or Vince and I, or Pat and Vince, or Pat and Vince and I, or sometimes just me alone, went down there to marvel and explore several times over the next few weeks. We weren't allowed to see Mr. Berrigan's finished products, but we liked them even better seeing them as works in progress.

The mayor, in the meantime, was fit to be tied. He couldn't shut the Whacks Museum down on an obscenity charge, and he couldn't sue Mr. Berrigan for libel or slander since the wax figure in the window was a tribute to His Honor. Of course most of the town was laughing at him, which was obviously but not *legally* Mr. Berrigan's intent. But Mayor Hubert came up with an idea and at the next council meeting he got up and introduced a measure to rezone Frémont Street so as to exclude shows and displays and businesses where merchandise is not purchased nor food consumed. The council, all his buddies and fellow cronies, of course passed the amendment unanimously, and Mr. Berrigan was informed the next day that he was in violation of the town zoning ordinance and had sixty days to vacate the premises of his wax figures. Of course, he could *sell* them, that would be within the spirit of the zoning change, but he couldn't charge anyone to just come in and *look* at them. He could've put price tags on them and *pretended* to sell them, but he still wouldn't be able to legally charge the admission fee.

Mr. Berrigan didn't have a leg to stand on. The proposed amendment was posted in the legal ads in the *Courier*, as was proper, and all parties in opposition were invited to attend the council meeting. Mr. Berrigan, as mentioned, never attended the council meetings, which were all open to the public, and no one else—all parents and Bellerive residents and PTA members—saw fit to rise in his defense. As Vince put it, Mr. Berrigan had been screwed, blued, and tattooed. In two months, he had to be out.

Our parents all reluctantly gave us one last dollar and let us go in to see the exhibits one more time. We all—us kids, I mean—told Mr. Berrigan how sorry we were, but he didn't say anything, just shrugged and shook his head. We knew how he loved that museum and all the statues, but we also knew that he wouldn't want to cry in front of a bunch of kids.

About six weeks after the council vote, the American Legion chapter had its annual dinner-dance at the Legion Hall, an ex-Masonic temple that was also used for most of the weddings and bar mitzvahs in town. Over a thousand people attended; the AL dinner-dance was *the* social event of the Bellerive calendar, since a sprinkling of everyone— the Protestants and the Catholics, the Jews and the blacks—all came together under one roof for friendly and patriotic socializing.

I wasn't there, of course, but the *Courier* the next day had the story in such graphic detail that I might as well have been:

People started drifting out between twelve thirty and one A.M. Among them was Mayor Hubert, flushed with the congratulations of a cross-section of Bellerive society for his masterful handling of the Whacks Museum affair. The mayor was crossing the gravel road that separated the Hall from the grass parking lot when all of a sudden this big black car—a Cadillac, by all witnesses' descriptions— comes zooming down the road, spitting rocks in all directions, and catches the mayor right when he's in the middle of the road. The impact sent him flying fifty feet, and he was dead before he hit the ground. The car kept speeding, didn't slow down, just made jelly out of poor Mr. Hubert and kept going.

But what made the story even more interesting was that as the "death car" (so named in the *Courier*) passed in front of the Legion Hall, spotlights used to illuminate the night shone directly into the vehicle, and no fewer than seventeen witnesses gave the exact same description of the driver. He was a middle-aged man, balding with a pronounced widow's peak, a good thirty or forty pounds overweight, with wireless glasses and a small mustache, like the one Gale Gordon on the *Our Miss Brooks* show wore. But what was more remarkable was that all the witnesses agreed that the driver had a look of fear or horror on his face, which he had *before* he hit the mayor, and which didn't change *after* he struck him. Speculation was that the guy's accelerator was stuck, he couldn't control the car or stop it, and after he accidentally hit Mr. Hubert, he panicked and just kept on going. The state police were asked to help in the investigation, but as of the afternoon paper there were no suspects and no leads. An artist's rendition of the driver appeared in newspapers all over the state, and even the network affiliate in Little Rock showed the picture. After all, Mr. Hubert was the mayor of a town.

Well! I can tell you that when Pat and I met the next day in Boston Alley, we had little else to talk about. We had small sympathy for the loss of the mayor, since he had cost us Berrigan's Whacks Museum, but still, a crime of such brazen audacity deserved punishment. We spent a long time coming up with appropriate torments for the perpetrator, influenced no doubt by, but surpassing some of, the exhibits in the building we sat against.

Pat's father worked for a local moving company, and so he knew that on the following day a big truck had been reserved to start taking Mr. Berrigan's statues to their new home—a dead storage warehouse two hundred miles away. Having run out of ways to punish the mayor's killer, we decided to take one last, loving tour through Mr. Berrigan's basement.

Things hadn't changed much down there in the past few weeks. It was as if Mr. Berrigan had given up creating those magnificent works of his, and who could blame him? In fact, the last few times we'd been there we'd seen virtually *no* changes of any kind. It'd been like walking into a photograph. But this time, something struck me immediately, something that was on the large table, amid the lumps of wax and unfinished heads and knives. I walked over to it, and picked up one of those cheap cardboard "periscopes" with two little mirrors that were going at the five-and-ten for ninety-nine cents. You could use them to peer over fences and around buildings without being seen by the enemy, which came in handy while we were playing *Man from U.N.C.L.E.* But what would Mr. Berrigan be doing with one of them?

Pat had walked over to the other side of the room, where a draped figure stood. "I don't remember seeing this," he stage-whispered to me.

"Neither do I," I whispered back.

"I'm gonna see what it is," Pat said, and he pulled at the tarpaulin.

It was the figure of a middle-aged man, overweight, balding, with glasses and a Gale Gordon mustache. The hands were out, as if grasping a steering wheel. The face was frozen in a rictus of shock and fear. I think I gasped, but I know for a fact that Pat yelled and stepped backward, tripping over his own feet and pulling the tarp completely off the figure. The statue tottered for a moment, then righted itself.

"Pat!" I hissed. "That looks like the guy who was driving the car that hit the mayor!"

Pat was still sitting on the floor. I could hear his heart pounding from across the basement. "Dummy can't drive no car, dummy!" he said.

I brandished the periscope. "No, but what if someone put the statue in the car to make it look like it was driving, and then sat on the floor and worked the gas and used this to see over the dashboard"—I paused to gulp a breath— "so he could see where to steer!"

"Are you saying—" Pat began, but then we both froze at the sound of rapid footsteps coming down the stairs.

"Who's there?" we heard Mr. Berrigan call. They were the first words we'd heard him say in weeks.

"Hide!" I breathed, and ducked behind some boxes and crates. I hoped Pat had found himself a place to hide, too, but the blood rushing through my eyes had sort of made everything black.

I heard the sound of adult feet hitting the stone floor of

the basement. "Who's there?" Mr. Berrigan asked. "Come out of there, I know you're here!"

I started to get up. After all, I was guilty only of trespass, not breaking and entering or burglary. Only later did it occur to me that Mr. Berrigan would have been better off with no witnesses to his culpability.

As I rose behind the cartons, I was facing the driving statue. Mr. Berrigan was between me and the statue, his back to me. I was about to say something when the wax figure with the horrified expression moved forward an inch. From somewhere behind it, a deep voice said, "Berrigan!"

He jumped, and so did I, but then I recognized the voice as the one Pat used when he was imitating his father. What was he up to?

"Berrigan!" the "statue" said again, and it moved forward another inch. "What you did was wrong! Turn yourself in!"

I almost said, "Pat, are you crazy?" but the words died in my throat. If he had an idea, let him go ahead with it.

I could see the hairs on Mr. Berrigan's neck stand up, along with a few on his head. "Wh-wh—" he said.

The wax figure's hands began to move up and down. "You can't get away with this," Pat's father's voice said. "You can't live with this. Turn yourself in!"

The figure moved forward another inch, and began to sway gently. Mr. Berrigan was gulping, choking, trying to form words. Finally, he managed to spit out a sentence: "He—he t-took you all away from me! He took you!"

"We are just wax, Berrigan," the driver said. "We are

nothing. You took a human life." The voice grew louder. "You've committed a grave sin, Berrigan! You made me help you! Go to the police, now! Turn yourself in!"

I'll be screwed, blued, and tattooed if Mr. Berrigan didn't fall to his knees right there on the floor and begin to beg the figure's forgiveness. I actually started to laugh, but he was babbling so he didn't hear me. One of the statue's arms pointed toward the staircase.

"Go!" Pat's father said. "Now!"

I couldn't believe it as I saw it happening, but Mr. Berrigan got himself up and dragged himself up the stairs and out the door, apologizing and babbling all the way.

The tension and fear and I don't know what were released in me then, and I burst into uncontrollable laughter. By the time I stopped, Pat was standing near me, his eyes wide. He was shaking.

"Oh," I said to him, "that was great." I put a hand out. "Slap me five, jive," I said.

He didn't slap me anything. He said, in a small voice, "I didn't do nothin'."

"What do you mean?" I asked. "You scared Mr. Berrigan into going to confess."

Pat gave a little shake of his head. "I told you, I didn't do nothin'."

We both turned and looked at the wax figure. Then we both bolted up the stairs and out the door and down the alley in the best Three Stooges tradition.

Because, you see, when we'd both turned to look at the wax statue . . . it smiled.

The Undertaker's Wedding

CHET WILLIAMSON

It's a shame you children never knew your grandpa. Oh, he was such a gentle man. Problem was, people confused his gentleness with sneakiness, I couldn't tell you why. Maybe not sneakiness exactly, but more like cowing, is that the word? Like a cowed animal always looking for somebody to hit it. He was shy, that was all, and gentle. And because of that people thought he was less than he was. Why, in other towns you'd have your undertakers being well thought of, town council members, maybe even mayors like over in Willow Creek, even if it *was* just for two years. But not here in town, not for Grandpa.

I suspect some folks thought he never should've been an undertaker, quiet and shy as he was. Nowadays so many undertakers are big, hearty, happy men with red faces and big hands that grab you when you shake 'em, like what they're doing had nothing to do with death. Oh, at the funerals they look serious and make their mouths go straight, but on the street you'd think they were salesmen from how most of them act.

Your grandpa, he wasn't like that. He was gentle. He said to me once that his were the last hands to touch them on the earth, and he wanted their last memories of this place to be good because if they went to Heaven they might tell the Lord of the kindnesses they'd had here and He might not be so hard on us. If they went to the other place, well, then those poor souls'd value Grandpa's last kindnesses all the more. In fact, he said it was the bad'uns needed his gentleness most of all, since they'd most of them had so little shown to them when they were alive.

But nobody knew he thought like that, not even me. Oh, I giggled with the other girls, and as hard as any of 'em when he'd walk by on the street, or when he sat near some of us in church. Only in church, of course, we couldn't giggle, could only make little faces at each other. It *was* funny at first, and a little scary. Sometimes we'd giggle loud just so's he could hear us, and he'd stick his head down between his shoulders and scurry away. And maybe one of the girls would say, "You better not let him hear you laugh, or he'll come to your house some night and *drag you away*!" And surely that'd make us giggle all the more, at the thought of the quiet, creepy old undertaker trying to do that, when we knew he'd jump if you said boo to him. It wasn't *him* that made it scary, but what he did when we'd think about it, burying people, getting them all ready and having to undress them and wash them and dress them and put them in their coffins. It didn't seem nice, it just seemed scary. And that's why, even when we were laughing, we still felt a little funny, leastways I did.

I don't like to say that I was special or any nicer, but after a while it wasn't much fun for me to laugh at him at all. It didn't seem right somehow, or maybe I just grew up a little faster than the others. But one May day we were all coming out of the soda parlor on Market Street—it's long gone now—and he was walking by. Well, some of the others started to giggle, and he turned red right off. And I just thought, he looks so nice, and he did, with a pressed white shirt and dark trousers and a pretty blue bow tie, his hair just so, like he'd come from the barber shop, and I could smell some nice aftershave lotion that smelled so cool in that hot sun. So I shushed the others real sharp, and they shut up fast. But the shush I made was so loud it startled him, and he stopped dead in his tracks and just looked at me like I'd been shushing him. He looked in that second just like a little boy looking up at his ma, ready to do whatever she asked. But of course I *hadn't* been shushing him, so I just smiled and nodded, not knowing what else to do. Then he smiled, such a tiny little smile like he thought a bigger one would break his face, and he gave a little nod back at me, and kept walking.

Well, the other girls had a heyday with that. They giggled at first, then when he was gone they laughed fit to bust, and started singing, "Emmy's got a boyfriend, Emmy's got a boyfriend," and dancing in a circle around me. Then they laughed some more, and one of them said,

"You be careful, Emmy, I hear he got real *cold* hands." I just got mad then and walked away, deciding I wasn't going to make no more fun of him. Why, he'd *smiled* at me, and smiled real nice, too.

The next time I saw the girls, they acted funny, like I might be mad at them. I was a little, I guess, but they said no more about the day before and neither did I, so we were friends again, and I sort of forgot about the whole thing.

That's why it was a big surprise, a few days later, when my daddy told me the undertaker'd come to see him in the store where he clerked, and asked for permission to come calling on me. Surprise, did I say? Why, I fairly flew into a frazzle when I heard, and when my daddy told me he'd said it was all right, I near cried. "Now, Emmy," my daddy said, patting my shoulder, "don't take on so. He's just coming to call, nothing more. If you don't like him, you don't have to see him again, I promise." I guess I must have looked pretty scared, because he went on. "He's a good man, Emmy. A quiet man, but a good'un."

I just nodded. He was coming Friday night, and I didn't say nothing to my chums about it, didn't want them to find out if I could help it. That day I was so nervous I couldn't eat a bite for supper, just sat at the table and watched my mother and daddy eat. Mother looked near as scared as me, though she was getting some food down. Only my daddy seemed like normal, and he'd look at me and give me a smile that told me not to worry, but I did, and I don't really know about what.

Along about seven o'clock he came up the walk, carrying a bunch of flowers. They were awfully pretty, and I got a little choked up, since this was the first time I'd ever had a caller and flowers, not being one of the prettiest girls in town. But then the idea hit me so queer, of an undertaker bringing flowers, and I knew it was stupid, but all I could think of was where he'd *got* them from. I still feel bad today when I think of how that nasty thought got into my head, like a harsh word you can never take back. He must have seen what was in my mind when he handed them to me because his face looked like I'd just cut him with a knife, and he was trying hard not to let the pain show. But I made myself smile, and took the flowers, and gave them to Mother, who looked a little queasy as she took them, but I don't think he noticed.

Thank the Lord my daddy had taken the evening off from clerking at the dry goods, for he did most of the talking, asking Grandpa whether he thought that rain was going to come, and what he thought of the Athletics' chances, and whether they'd ever get a dam built up at French Creek. And Grandpa answered him soft and polite. It was the first time I'd ever heard him speak, and I was surprised at what a deep low voice he had, when I'd expected a high little peep. Not that he was small—he was a medium-sized man, I suppose—but he was just so shy and scary that you'd have thought he'd have the same kind of voice. Oh, it was shy, but low and real full, like I thought Lawrence Tibbett would sound if I'd ever heard him talk instead of sing.

After a while of talking, Daddy looked at me and smiled and then looked at my mother and said as how it was time to leave the young folks alone for a spell to get acquainted.

Well, that froze me a little, though not as cold as it would've before we'd all chatted for a while. So Mother and Daddy left us alone in our little front parlor and went back into the kitchen, where I could hear Daddy turning the pages of the newspaper and Mother saying things real low every once in a long while.

For the longest time Grandpa and I just sat there, he on the old wing chair, me across the room in a side chair with Mother's needlework on the seat and back. Neither one of us said a word, and finally he cleared his throat and said as how it was a real pleasure to be able to come and call on me, and he was wondering if I enjoyed the moving pictures. I allowed as how I did, and then he asked me if I would be interested in accompanying him—that's the word he used, *accompanying*—to the U.S. Theater the next night to see *The Old Homestead*. He told me it was a very respectable picture, and that Pastor Myers had seen it and said it was very good.

I didn't want to go, not really, but right then and there I was just so flustered that I didn't know how to make up a lie. Boys just didn't ask me out, not even boys I didn't want to go out with, and I had no experience with such things. So I just nodded and said all right, and he got the sweetest, happiest smile on his face that right off I was *glad* I'd said yes. Then he just talked a little more about the movie and took a little handout thing the theater gave away about it and handed it to me to keep, and I allowed that it looked like a good picture and we just sat there again until he remarked how late it was getting, and said he'd best be going. So I called Mother and Daddy out and we all said our good nights.

After he was gone, I didn't say anything to them and they asked me no questions, just eyed me, my mother worried-looking, Daddy smiling, and I excused myself and went upstairs.

Once I realized what I'd done, I got sort of panicked. I knew that my friends would be at the pictures, some of them anyway, and by next morning it'd be all over town that I'd been out with the undertaker. *Everybody'd* know at the service. And what about the service—would he expect me to sit with him? I had such foolish, awful dreams that night, I can still remember. Dreamt I was at the pictures with Grandpa, but the movie wasn't a real movie—it was Grandpa working, getting the dead ready for burial. And all around me my friends were watching and smiling at me and saying what a fine job he was doing, and though I couldn't bear to watch the screen, I couldn't *not* watch, either. Then Grandpa took my hand in the dark theater, and it was cold, so cold I woke up, to find my own hand grabbing the cool brass bedpost.

Next morning I told my daddy that I'd been asked out and said yes, but I wasn't sure I wanted to go. He said to me, well, you said you would, didn't you? And I allowed as how I had, and he said, well then, you should. Mother took my side, but Daddy said if she said she would, then she should. Next time just say no if you don't want to. You've got a mouth, so start to use it. Then he spoke less sharp and touched a hand to my cheek. He's a kind man, Emmy, he said. He said, he won't hurt you at all, but you be careful so's not to hurt him.

I knew he was right about going, and that night

Grandpa came by for me and we went to the pictures. I didn't see anyone I knew when we went in, and I felt ashamed that I was glad of it. The movie was good. It was the first time I ever heard Grandpa laugh, and such a sweet laugh he had, like music. He never touched my hand once, nor put an arm around me.

When the show was over and the lights came on, I saw Mandy Dawson sitting two rows back with her fellow, looking at me like the cat that just ate the bird, and I knew she'd start spreading the news that very night. There was something in her look that right then made me mad, made me think the hell with what *they* think. I know that's no language for a lady, but that's what went through my head, and when Grandpa asked if I'd like a soda, I smiled and said yes, and we went in the soda parlor and sat at a bright table in front where any nosy parker could see us, and talked about the movie and a lot more, and we *both* smiled that night.

Next morning I sat with him in church, and I think it surprised my mother as much as it did my friends. Oh, they gave me the dirt at first, but once they knew that I'd see who I *wanted* to see, they left me be quick enough. Some of them left me be for good, though my best friends stuck by me—Marion and Dorothy and Katie. In fact, they confessed that they'd always thought Grandpa was sort of cute, no matter what he did.

He and I didn't talk about that for the longest time, even though we started going together regular. He lived above the funeral parlor, and of course I never went over there anyway, that just wasn't done. When we'd have plans to do something, and someone would die and he'd have to hold the service and all, he'd just say he was sorry but we couldn't go to so and so because he was needed. That's what he'd say, he was needed. And I'd know, and it would be all right. But we never talked about it directly. Leastways, not till he asked me to marry him.

We'd been going out together for maybe five months when he got up the nerve. It was October, and we'd just been on a hayride with the church, and he was walking me home, and he stopped right on the corner of Orange Street and Washington, and he asked me if I'd consider being his wife. It was pretty chilly that October, but that wasn't why I shivered so. And don't go thinking I shivered because it was the *undertaker* asking me to wed him. I shivered because marrying him had been all I'd been thinking about since we went to the soda parlor after that first picture. I loved that man sure enough, but if you'd told me I'd be feeling that way six months earlier, I'd've called you crazy.

But I didn't say yes right away. Maybe I would've if he'd let me go, but straightaway after he asked me he told me to take my time and think about it. I said I would, but I smiled so, and kissed him on the cheek, that he knew fairly well what my answer would be. Once we got to my house we didn't go straight in but sat on the porch swing in that autumn chill and talked real low so's my mother and daddy wouldn't hear.

He told me a lot about himself I'd never heard before, how he'd become an undertaker because his daddy had been one and it was the only thing he'd been taught, how his daddy had died when he was nineteen and he'd taken over the undertaking parlor but folks were hesitant to trust their dead to someone that young so he had a hard few years. He never made many friends because he was too busy working at odd jobs he had to do to be able to live. When the Spanish-American War came along, he enlisted, and when he came back to town, folks were more likely to use his services because, he said, then folks thought he was a man since he'd been to war. And he shook his head, his eyes real sad.

He didn't say anything for a while. Then he said he liked what he did, and made no apology to any man for it. It was something that had to be done, just like doctoring or governing, or being a fireman or policeman, something that helped folks. It was then he told me what I said before, about kindness and gentleness being the last things done to them, and I got a little bit weepy when he said that, thinking what a scary old monster we girls had made him out to be. Last, he told me how old he was. Forty. I was nineteen. But it didn't matter any. I told him I'd marry him, and then I kissed him on the lips for the first time. They were warm and dry and soft, just the way I'd always thought a husband's lips should be.

The next day he asked Daddy for my hand, and Daddy said yes. By that time Mother knew Grandpa well enough to know what a good man I was getting. But even I didn't know how good he really was. I found out that winter.

It was a monstrous cold winter. We had our first big snow in mid-November, and it must have been two feet deep at least. It never got warm enough to melt it until early March, so snow piled on top of snow, and it just got deeper and deeper. The roads stayed open, though. Seemed every time you looked, the Hastings boys were out plowing them. Don't know how much the town paid them that winter, but the next spring both Dick and Bob started new houses. Grandpa had a hard time, too. The ground was frozen solid, and the Hastings boys, who also dug the graves at the Upper and Lower Dellfield cemeteries, nearly doubled their price because of it. Grandpa once told me he'd probably paid for their chimneys that winter. He wouldn't pass on the extra price to his customers, though. Claimed that a loved one's death was bad luck enough, so the freeze was *his* bad luck.

But it wasn't because of the snows alone that folks remembered that winter. Twenty years later you'd mention that winter and folks'd say wasn't that the year Roy Stoller got killed trying to rob the feed store? It wasn't often that things like that would happen, even in *Lower* Dellfield. First shooting death, my daddy said, since Amos Martin accidentally killed his cousin Wilbur when they were hunting back in '03. I don't think it surprised anyone, though, leastways not anyone who knew about Roy Stoller. Roy was a bad'un, no two ways about it. He just seemed doomed for something like that to happen. His daddy was mostly no-account, and his mother died when he was born. Roy quit his schooling when he was only ten to help his daddy try to pull some harvest out of that scrubby ten acres they called a farm. Now, I expect, that ten acres would fetch a fair price, but back then it was worthless. After old Mr. Stoller died, Roy gave up farming and just lived there in the farmhouse, tending a little vegetable patch and keeping mostly to himself, except when he'd come into town for supplies, or to drink at Rohrer's Tavern. Nobody knew for sure where he got the money he needed, but there'd been some talk of insurance money on his daddy, and some folks said he stole. They were proved right, of course. He spent a few days in jail, on and off, especially after drinking nights, mostly from picking fights in the tavern. Had no friends, none at all. People didn't like him much and seemed to stay away.

A couple of weeks after Christmas he broke into the feed store through a back window. He didn't know Mr. Wenger was working late in in his office, and Mr. Wenger surprised him with a pistol. Roy Stoller had a gun, too, and shot first but missed. Then Mr. Wenger shot Roy right in the head. The doc said he was dead before he hit the floor.

There were no relatives and no estate to speak of, so the county was supposed to pay a local undertaker fifty dollars to bury him. The sheriff took him to Frank Weyden first, but Weyden wouldn't do it—said it'd be bad for his business, handling criminals. But Grandpa said he'd take Roy, and next day when he told me he'd done it I didn't like it, but I didn't say anything except something about the fifty dollars being a small price to get for tarnishing his business.

He got real serious then, as near to mad as I'd ever seen him before or since, and told me that no matter what folks'd done, it wasn't ours to judge them once they were dead, but rather to give them as much dignity and kindness as we could, for they'd be judged quick enough by someone far higher. Then he said Roy Stoller'd never had a chance for anything in his life, and how he was more to be pitied than anything else. His words made me feel pretty small, though I was still concerned with what other folks might think. But that didn't bother Grandpa in the least, and he even gave back to the county what was left of the fifty dollars after he'd paid his costs on the coffin and the grave digging. I won't profit off an unfortunate, he said, and nobody was more unfortunate than Roy Stoller. Grandpa put him next to his daddy, in the Lower Dellfield Cemetery. At the funeral, there was just him and me and the Negro pastor from the Baptist church over in West Davis. The Dellfield ministers were all busy that day, so they said.

We got married in early February, a week after my twentieth birthday. We hadn't had snow for almost two weeks, and the sun was shining bright as anything. The temperature was just below freezing, and after the winter we'd been through, it felt like the South Seas. It was just a small wedding. I only invited my closest friends and their families. Since Grandpa had no real friends to speak of, I made sure Mother had the two ushers seat some of the guests on the groom's side. Grandpa looked handsome, and the mirror told me I was as pretty as I was ever going to be, and it was a nice wedding. Although at the end of the vows, when we said till death us do part, I got that funny feeling again—it just came over me—and I wondered if I died first, if he'd take care of me, make me ready for the grave.

It was a dark thought, and it had no place at a happy thing like a wedding, so right then I drove it out of my head. But I thought about it for a long time afterward.

We had the reception in the church basement, and my daddy and mother were both happy but teary-eyed.

Grandpa was chattering away with the guests and members of the wedding, just like he'd never been shy in his life, and I remember thinking, well Jiminy Christmas, this man should've got married a long time ago. Some of the people there that day became his friends for life.

I'd asked him and asked him where we were to go on our honeymoon, but he wouldn't tell me. A surprise, was all he'd say. But no Niagara Falls, or anything like that. Somewhere that we can *keep*, he whispered, and I just couldn't work out what he meant.

After the reception we went back to my daddy's house to pick up my suitcase, and then we climbed into Grandpa's Model T, and off we went, out of Upper Dellfield, and through Lower Dellfield, then up into the hills north of here, which surprised me. All the cities and towns of any size are all east and south, but we headed north instead. I said as how I hoped we'd get to where we were going before too long, as night was coming on and the sky had turned dark like there was snow coming. Don't worry, he told me, we're almost there now. And sure enough in another mile he turned the car up this dirt road smack dab through the woods. It looked like it had just been plowed that day, for you could see the brown earth in patches through the snow. Looks like the Hastings boys made it, he said, and I asked him just what was going on here, and he said you'll see.

Finally we came to a spot where the lane ended and the trees got too thick for an automobile to pass. We walk from here, he said, and lifted me out of the car. Then he took two pairs of snowshoes from the back of the Model

T, and I just looked at him. He asked me if I'd ever walked on them before, and of course I hadn't, so he showed me how. I was still asking him what it was all about but he wouldn't tell me, just picked up my suitcase and his and asked me to follow him. Whither thou goest, he said, and laughed.

By that time it was nearly dark, and it had started to snow as well, big wet flakes that looked like white leaves falling in the dusk. We followed a little trail through the trees, and I could see other snowshoe tracks, so I asked whose they were. Grandpa said they were his.

It was just light enough so we didn't need a lantern when we got to the cabin. It was in a little open space in the woods, and a small stream solid with ice was next to it. It was the prettiest little building I'd ever seen, made of light brown logs. There was a black shingle roof and a green door and shutters, and mostly covered with snow as it was, it looked like something from a fairy tale. I felt Grandpa's arm around my shoulders, and he asked me if I liked it. There was no doubt of that. I thought there couldn't have been a better place in the world for two people who loved each other to be alone. He told me his father had built it years before, but after he died Grandpa rented it to an old trapper who finally had to give up his line that past year because of his legs and move in with relatives. Grandpa'd been coming up here for months fixing it up as a surprise for me.

I hugged him hard and told him I couldn't wait to see inside, so we tramped the rest of the way through the snow, which was falling thicker now, and went inside and lit a lantern. It was beautiful. He'd put curtains at all the windows and hung some pictures on the walls. At one end was a little table with two chairs, a dry sink, and a woodstove, with cupboards full of dishes and food. There were three chairs and a fireplace in the middle of the room, and at the other end was a chest of drawers and a bed behind a big red curtain he'd rigged up so as to give me my privacy. But right then I didn't want any privacy, not from him anyway. I hugged him and kissed him and said as how it would be a wonderful honeymoon, and he laughed that gentle low laugh and said it would be if we didn't freeze first.

He took the lantern over to the big open fireplace and touched a match to the kindling he'd got ready before. It caught fast and started crackling and popping for fair. It must have been a pine knot or something like it that cracked so loud and threw a hot spark into the lantern, but at the time I could've sworn it was a bomb. The lantern just exploded—I didn't see it, just heard it—and when I turned around and looked, Grandpa was falling over like a big tree, and fire was jumping all over the wooden floor. I didn't bother to scream, but yanked down the curtain and started beating out the fire with it. It didn't take long, and then I looked at Grandpa. He'd been scarcely singed, but a piece of that thick, heavy glass from the lantern's base had hit him right on the temple, cutting him open and making him bleed something fierce. He wasn't conscious, either.

I ripped a hunk out of my slip and tried to stop the blood, but it kept coming, slow and steady, and I knew that I had to get him to a doctor fast. I thought of dragging him out to the car on a blanket, but even if I could do it, the jolting might do him worse than leaving him be.

We had only the one lantern, so by the light of the fire I lit some candles, then pressed down on Grandpa's cut and tried to think. It was dark as pitch now, and the snow was falling so thick and the wind blowing so hard it seemed the cabin's roof might blow clean off. There was no way I could get him out, and I wondered if I could find the way out myself, and bring back help. I thought as how that was the only way I could save him, so I put some logs on the fire to keep him warm, tied a bandage tight around his head, bundled myself up as much as I could, and went outside on the snowshoes.

I hadn't gone twenty yards before I knew it was impossible. Even if the trail had been plain in front of me, I couldn't have seen it. So I turned around and made my way back to the cabin, following the little glow of the fire through the windows. Grandpa was no better, still unconscious, though the bleeding had slowed a little. But his breathing was real funny, and I don't mind telling you children I was scared more than I'd ever been, being purely certain he'd die before I could ever get out and maybe bring back somebody the next day.

All I could do was sit there on the floor, holding his poor bleeding head in my lap, and pray. I prayed that night like Jesus must have prayed in the garden. And I'm not sure if God heard me or not, but I know something did. For sometime in that long night, I heard through the wind a knocking on the cabin door. No footsteps on the boards of the porch, but just a knocking. Three times, real slowlike.

I didn't even think. I just ran to the door and flung it

open, and I saw Roy Stoller standing there on the porch.

I knew it was him. I'd seen his face before, and it looked fairly as it must have when he was alive. You'll remember the winter had been cold and the ground was frozen. So what was under the ground stayed frozen, too. I could still see the little mark in his forehead where Grandpa had closed up the bullet hole. And the firelight was bright enough that I recognized the old suit of Grandpa's that he'd dressed him in.

I didn't scream. I think I was too scared to. I just stepped back, and Roy Stoller walked into the cabin, went over to Grandpa, and picked him up as lightly as if he were a child. Then he walked to the cabin door with him, and turned and looked at me, like he was waiting. And something in his dead face told me that it was *good* he wanted to do, not bad. So I bundled up again and put on the snowshoes, and though it took all my courage to do it, I wrapped a blanket around Grandpa as he lay in Roy Stoller's arms. Then Roy Stoller walked out the door into the storm, and I followed him.

He didn't glow or nothing, and he didn't talk at all, but I had no trouble following him, even though I couldn't see him. It was like there was some kind of warmth coming from him, and I just followed it. Before too long we were at the car, and Roy Stoller put Grandpa in the back. I just stood there, not knowing what to do next. I'd never driven a car, only ridden in one since I'd been going with Grandpa. So Roy Stoller got it started right up and got in the driver's side, while I climbed into the back with Grandpa. I wondered how we'd get through the snow—

about a foot had fallen, and you couldn't even see the lane we'd come in on—but that didn't worry Roy Stoller none. The automobile just seemed to drift over the snow, and when I looked behind, I couldn't see any tracks we'd made.

We drove for what seemed like ages, passing nary another automobile, though that snow was so thick we wouldn't have seen another car's lights even if anyone had been foolish enough to be out that night. Finally the Model T slowed down and just *floated* to a stop, and I swear I could feel it and us sink slowly and softly into the deep snow on the ground. Roy Stoller didn't do anything, just sat there looking out into the night like he'd done all he could. I looked out to the right and saw a dim light glowing, so I climbed out of the car and walked through the snow toward it. I was just amazed when I saw where I was—right in the middle of town, and that glowing light was a lamp in Doc Farnsworth's window.

I pounded on the door till Doc's wife opened it and called her husband down from upstairs. I took him by the hand and led him out to the automobile, not even wondering what Doc would do when he saw dead Roy Stoller sitting behind the wheel, only worrying about Grandpa and wanting to get him into the warm as quick as could be. But Roy Stoller wasn't in the car anyway, and when Doc was hauling Grandpa up onto his shoulders, I looked out into the dark but couldn't see him anywhere. There was no tracks of his walking away, either, though even if there had been the wind might've blown them away just that quick. But I don't think there were.

You children all know that Grandpa *didn't* die. He came

to the next day, and Doc said it'd been a good thing I got Grandpa to him when I did, that he just might have bled to death. It was peculiar. From the second Roy Stoller picked Grandpa up in his arms, the bleeding stopped. But soon as Doc took him from the car, I could see it had started again. Of course Doc got it stopped fast once we were inside. He knew how.

When Grandpa woke up and realized where he was, he asked me how I did it, how I got him back to town, and so I told him about Roy Stoller. I wasn't sure, and I'm still not sure to this day, whether he believed me or not, because he smiled a smile that could've meant he thought I was seeing things, or likewise it might've been a smile he smiled because he knew he'd been right about the way he thought about and treated the dead folks.

A few days later, when he was up and around and the snow had long since stopped, we went down to the Lower Dellfield Cemetery and looked at Roy Stoller's grave. It was under the snow same as the rest, and when Grandpa brushed the snow away to see the earth beneath, it looked like any fresh grave, with no sign that anything'd come out of it. But still, that wasn't proof that something hadn't. There was nothing else at the grave—no piece of the blanket I'd wrapped around Grandpa or any of the clues you'd expect to find in a real old-fashioned ghost story. Just the snow and the hard earth. I left some flowers I'd brought along. Roses. They looked real pretty on the white snow. And I hoped as we walked away that maybe what Roy Stoller'd done that night would help to make up for the bad he'd done when he was alive. The more I thought about it, the more I was sure that it should just plumb *erase* that badness, wipe it away. For all he'd done, Roy Stoller'd never *killed* anybody, but he did save a life, and I was mighty thankful to him for it.

I was thankful, too, that Grandpa was the man he was, that he'd done good for Roy Stoller from his heart. At first I'd thought that what he'd said about kindness to the dead was nice but foolish. But now I know better. It wasn't ever too late to be kind. And you can be kind even to people's memories, and it might be known to them, and appreciated. Grandpa taught me that lesson. He taught me other things, too, and he taught me good. Why, you children can just look at yourselves if you don't believe me.

Oh, I hope you don't mind me calling you children, but that's how I think of you, especially since Grandpa and I never had any of our own. It just seemed natural for us to call *you* our children. After all, we care for you, comfort you, lay you down in your last sleep.

There now. All finished, and all ready. That wasn't bad, was it? I just wish Grandpa was still alive to see how peaceful you look. Yes, peaceful. I may not be the best or the fanciest undertaker in these parts, but I dare hope to say I'm the most gentle.

Old Flame

Taylor McCafferty

After a funeral you're supposed to feel sad. And maybe a little scared, after coming face to face with the finality of death and all. I don't think, however, that you're supposed to feel angry, but that's what I feel, all right. Real angry. With nobody left to be mad at anymore. Except maybe Pa.

I'm sitting out here on the front porch, and I can hear him real plain in the kitchen, sniffling. Everybody that came by to pay their respects has finally gone, and Pa's out there, rattling pots and pans, like maybe he's going to make us something to eat.

Now *that* would be a first. Pa, cooking. He's just making all that noise so I'll hear him and get up and fix something for us. In a minute he'll be yelling at me, "Ida Sue, ain't it about time for dinner?" How he can even think about eating is beyond me.

And all that pan rattling out there sure doesn't cover up his sniffling. I'm trying to keep calm, but that sniffling is a real irritating thing to have to listen to.

Because I know Pa's just crying for Jenelle. Not for anybody else. Not for me, not Chandler. Just Jenelle. I know Pa blames me for all this, too. I can see it in his eyes. And, of course, I can't forget what he screamed at me that day.

I know Pa won't ever admit the part he played in all this, either. After all, he did start it, didn't he? If he hadn't spoiled Jenelle so bad, giving her everything she ever wanted, maybe things would've been different. And if Pa hadn't ever told us how our mama really died, maybe none of this would've happened. Part of being able to do a thing is believing you can do it, isn't it? And Papa helped me and Jenelle with the believing part. He helped us with that real good.

I was just thirteen the day Pa decided to break the news. Jenelle was fourteen; and if there was such a thing as a line between pretty and beautiful, Jenelle had crossed it that year. She made you want to gasp just looking at her.

I admit it, back then I couldn't help being jealous of her. Pa had been worshiping at her feet ever since she was a baby. And my mirror plainly told me she had me beat real bad in the looks department. Jenelle had long, wavy, chestnut-colored hair, creamy-white skin, and big blue eyes with lashes so thick they looked false. At fourteen she had the kind of figure grown women envy.

I, on the other hand, had the kind of figure they call

skinny, and the kind of hair they call dishwater blonde. It was real limp, too, like maybe some of that dishwater had been left in it.

It didn't help any, either, to know that your father plain and simple liked your sister best. Who was it that Pa put his arm around while he was telling us about Mama? Jenelle, of course. I was standing right next to him, too, but Pa reached over and pulled Jenelle close.

"Now, Jenelle, Ida Sue," he said, "it's high time you two finally knew about what happened to your mama. And I want to be the one to tell you before you hear it from somebody else."

To this day I'm still not sure why Pa told us. Neither Jenelle nor I even remembered our mama. She'd died when I was still a baby. And it wasn't like we still lived in Pigeon Fork where it all happened. We'd moved from there to Bullitt Lick right after Mama died. And nobody here even knew about it. Or if they'd heard about it long ago, they never connected the story to us.

Still, Jenelle was starting high school the next week. Maybe Pa was afraid she would look it all up in the high school library. I'd heard tell that the new library the high school had just built had years of back issues of a dozen Kentucky newspapers. So maybe Pa was worried. Because even though Pigeon Fork was a hundred miles away, Mama had made news statewide.

I can still remember the way Pa's voice dropped to a whisper when he told us. Like he was talking about something sacred. Or maybe something too frightening to talk about out loud.

"Your mama was sitting out on the back porch swing, holding her cat Muffin on her lap. I was in the kitchen, right on the other side of the screen door. So I could see her real plain out there, staring straight ahead, swinging back and forth. She was in a snit about something or another." Here Pa's eyes dropped for a second.

Even at thirteen I could guess what Mama might've been mad about. As far back as I could remember Pa had been something of a ladies' man; he was real good-looking, dark and slim—and he must've dated every available woman around these parts. And he even dated some that weren't available. Both Jenelle and I had heard the gossip about Pa. In a town the size of Bullitt Lick, you couldn't keep something like that a secret. Jenelle and I exchanged a knowing look before Pa went on.

"She was just sitting, with that dang cat of hers. Then, all of a sudden, as sure as I'm sitting here, your mama just burned up."

Jenelle and I looked at him for a second without saying a word. Then I asked, my voice shaking a little, "What do you mean, burned up?"

"I mean, she just caught fire. That's all." Pa's eyes got this haunted look in them. "I—I tried to save her. I ran out there, thinking I'd get her to roll on the ground, like you're supposed to do. But you couldn't get near her. She was all blue flame." Pa's voice trailed off. "Just blue flame is all."

Jenelle's eyes were even bigger than usual now. She swallowed once, and then asked, "Was she sitting by a stove?" Now, you've got to understand here that while Jenelle may have been heavy on looks, she was a quart low on smarts. Pa was used to it by now, though. All he did was take a deep breath before he answered her.

"I said your ma was out on the porch, Jenelle. There aren't too many stoves out on a porch." Pa's voice was slow and patient. He rubbed his hand over his eyes like he was trying to rub the memory away. "That was what was so weird. The fire looked like it was coming from *inside* her."

Jenelle's eyes seemed to fill her whole face. Me, I was trying real hard not to smile. Because I was thinking, you mean to tell me that all these years we've been told that our mama died in a fire, and now you expect us to believe that Mama *was* the fire? Right.

"What happened to the cat?" My voice must've sounded a little skeptical, because Pa gave me a sharp glance.

"Now look, little girl," he said, "I'm trying to warn you. The same thing happened to that cat as happened to your mama, and I don't want it happening again. Ever." Pa looked away then, scowling. When he spoke again, his voice was real low, almost as if he were talking to himself. "You know, that porch swing she was sitting on wasn't even singed. Or the floor around them. But your mama—" Pa actually shuddered. He got up then, real abrupt. "Look, I don't ever want to talk about it again. I felt like you two should know. That's all."

Then he went on into the living room, and started reading the paper. Like what he'd just told us about wasn't anything more interesting than what happened at the church social last week.

After Pa went inside, Jenelle wrinkled her pretty nose and said, "Well, that was a disgusting thing for him to tell us. Yuck."

Seeing my big strong father actually shudder had done a lot to convince me that Pa was telling us the truth. "I think he was trying to warn us," I said.

"About what? I think he was being mean, telling us a creepy thing like that." Jenelle was pouting by then, so I gave up trying to talk to her.

In fact, we didn't talk about it for a long time after that. I thought about it, though, wondering about poor Mama. Sometimes I even cried for her—for that woman I never got to know. But every time I'd start to bring it up with Jenelle, she'd cut me off with, "Look, that's disgusting, okay?" And she'd flounce out of the room.

The next year when I started high school myself, I looked it all up in the library. Sure enough, Mama was written up in a lot of papers. All of them called it the same thing. Spontaneous human combustion. Like the way oily rags catch fire in a shed sometimes. Those newspapers said that there have been quite a few people over the years who've died like that. The papers said there's a lot in your body that could catch fire, like fats and oils, phosphorus, stuff like that.

After I read all those articles about Mama, it all seemed more real to me. More real, and more frightening. I started thinking about it a lot. Thinking about how they say your brain operates by making electrical connections. Like tiny sparks in your brain. I figured maybe what happened to Mama was like that. Maybe she got so upset that day that one of those brain sparks got out of control—and it caught her on fire.

I tried again to tell Jenelle about it, too. "We'd better be careful," I said, "because you can never tell. Maybe we're like Mama, and if we get too upset, it could happen to us, too."

Jenelle looked real pale for a minute. Then she shrugged and tossed her dark curls. "Look, our mama made an ash of herself a long time ago." She smiled at her little joke. "It's got nothing to do with us."

I tried to make her listen, but she wouldn't hear of it. Eventually I realized Jenelle probably had nothing to worry about anyway. Because everything she wanted she seemed to get. Looking at her perfect face and perfect figure, I decided it was real likely that Jenelle might live her whole life and never once get upset.

It was me that had to be careful.

So I worked on getting to be real easygoing. About everything. When I'd forget to do one of my chores—and Jenelle would tell Pa—I learned to just keep cool. It got to where I could stand there and have Pa yell at me right in front of Jenelle, and I wouldn't feel a thing. Even when Jenelle made up stuff that I did, and she'd stand there, with that little half-smile on her face, all the time Pa was smacking me. Nothing was worth dying over, so I got laid back. After a while there wasn't anything in the world that I cared about enough to get upset over.

Until I met Chandler Farris. Chandler had just transferred to our high school in my freshman year, and even though he was a year ahead of me, we were assigned to the same study hall.

I noticed him the first day he walked in. Chandler wasn't exactly the handsomest guy I'd ever seen, but he had the kind of face you don't get tired of looking at. Blue eyes, freckled nose, easy smile. A shock of sandy hair always falling in his eyes. I guess I was in love the minute I saw him, sitting across from me. When he asked me out, I thought I might actually faint from happiness.

When he asked me to go steady, I practically did faint. I guess those months I went steady with Chandler were the happiest I've ever known. Before or since. Suddenly, it didn't matter if the phone rang constantly for Jenelle, or if Pa practically ignored me, or anything else. I had Chandler, and that was all I needed.

I couldn't believe how lucky I was. One night driving home from the movies in Chandler's old Ford, he kept looking over at me and smiling. And looking over at me and smiling some more. Finally, I said, "What is it?"

That's when he told me. "You know what I really like about you?"

I shook my head no. It was the truth. I really had no idea.

"You're pretty and you don't know it."

I must've turned bright red. Chandler reached over and took my hand. For a minute we just grinned at each other.

"You're real smart, too." Now, I wasn't sure about that, either. Oh, I made good grades, all right. But if you never went out on dates—and before Chandler, I didn't—then you had a lot of time to study.

My grades didn't suffer any when I started dating Chandler, either. Because Chandler was a real serious student, too. He wanted to be a doctor, so he studied as much as I did. A lot of times we studied together. Jenelle used to laugh at us, calling us "the bookworms," like it was a dirty word. But that was before Chandler won that award in his junior year.

We'd been going together about a year when Chandler got selected something called a "President's Scholar." It's a big honor around here. It got Chandler's picture in the paper; it got him a full scholarship at any Kentucky college; and, let's face it, it got him Jenelle.

I'll never forget the expression on Jenelle's face while she read about Chandler in the Bullitt Lick *Gazette*. It was like watching a cat read about a mouse. I remember feeling real uneasy, watching her face.

Pa was impressed with Chandler, too. He took that paper right out of Jenelle's hands and said, "This here boy's going to be rich one day. You mark my words. Rich." He beamed at me the whole time he was talking. It was probably the first time he'd ever said an approving thing to me.

Jenelle looked like she'd been slapped. She didn't look any better when Pa went on, "Jenelle, you'd do good to find yourself a catch like Ida Sue has. Somebody who's going to have some money. Instead of all those football idiots you're always mooning over." Jenelle had just started going steady with yet another football idiot that week; she turned without a word and stomped out of the room.

Up to then Jenelle had made it a point not to be around when "The Drip"—that's what she called Chandler—came around. But after that little scene with Pa, she was suddenly hanging all over Chandler the minute he walked in the door.

The first time she did it, I got as mad as I could let myself get. "He's mine, Jenelle," I told her as soon as Chandler left.

Jenelle gave me a look that said, "Oh, yeah?" Her mouth said, "All's fair in love and war." And she gave me one of those little half-smiles of hers as she walked away.

I watched her, feeling a little sick. And Chandler. Poor Chandler. He never knew what hit him. Even today it seems as if one day he was mine, and the next day I walked into the living room and saw them. Jenelle and Chandler, wrapped in each other's arms, so close together they seemed to be one.

I'd seen it coming by then, of course. I couldn't help but notice the new dazed look Chandler was wearing lately. Or how all of a sudden Jenelle seemed to need Chandler's help with every subject she had. I also noticed how Jenelle's hand lingered on his when she handed him her school-book, or got him a Coke. How she was always leaning real close to him so he could smell all that perfume she wore.

I could see it happening, all right, but I didn't know how to stop it. How could somebody like me fight somebody like Jenelle?

It must've taken Jenelle a little time to take Chandler away from me, but it seemed like fifteen minutes. Max. After I walked in on them that night, I just stood there, not wanting to believe my eyes. For a second I couldn't breathe. My heart started pounding real funny, and my face got real hot. Jenelle and Chandler both started talking at once. Chandler was almost stammering. "Oh, Ida Sue, I am so sorry. Jenelle and I—we—"

I didn't wait around to hear the rest. I just turned and ran upstairs as fast as I could. There I took a long, long shower, standing under the cool water and crying and crying. Until finally I was all cried out. Finally, I'd washed that awful scene right out of my mind.

I never broke down again. After that, when Chandler started coming by to pick up Jenelle, I made sure I was out of sight. I still watched him, though, from behind the curtains in my room. Watched him going off with Jenelle, smiling into her eyes. I wanted to hate him, but I just couldn't. Hating Jenelle, however, was real easy.

When Chandler went away to Centreville College that next year, I didn't know which hurt the most—seeing him with Jenelle or not seeing him at all.

Before he left, Chandler and Jenelle got engaged. Jenelle showed me that diamond ring just like I'd never dated Chandler myself. Like he'd always been hers. It was as if she'd put the whole thing out of her mind. "I think Chandler and I were meant for each other," Jenelle told me. She actually told me that.

After Chandler left for college, Jenelle moped around the house for about two weeks. Pa started complaining weakly about her running up a phone bill calling Chandler long distance.

Then, of course, Jenelle couldn't sit at home. She started dating other guys.

"Jenelle, what are you doing? What about Chandler?" I asked her the first time she went flouncing out of the house with some guy she'd met at the restaurant where she'd started working.

Jenelle looked at me as cool as you please. "What about him?" she said.

I couldn't think of a thing to say back to her. I just stared at her, open-mouthed.

She shrugged, and smiled that little half-smile of hers.

"Now don't get all uppity with me, Ida Sue. I still love Chandler just like always. He's going to give me everything I've ever wanted. But *he* wouldn't want me sitting around this house getting bored. There's no harm in me having a little fun."

I had to clench my hands together to keep from slapping her. I thought about telling Chandler, too. But I knew he wouldn't believe me, or else he'd hate me for trying to stir up trouble. So I kept still. And waited.

That was during my senior year in high school. To keep my cool, I buried myself in my studies. I ended up with straight A's and a full scholarship. To any college I wanted. That fall I decided to go to Centreville College, just like Chandler.

I guess in the back of my mind I knew what I was up to. That what finally happened I'd planned all along. But I told myself that I was going to Centreville just to be near Chandler, that was all. I realized he belonged to Jenelle now, but I just wanted to see him again. Nothing more. Just to see him.

I think I believed that. I know it never occurred to Jenelle I could be going to Centreville because of Chandler. For one thing, Jenelle could never think of me as competition. I'd filled out some, and I'd learned to wear makeup right; but Jenelle had me beat so long ago, I don't think she even saw me anymore.

As a matter of fact, the day before I left, Jenelle actually gave me a hug and said, "Now you keep an eye on my man. Make sure he doesn't get away from me." Then she laughed like the idea was preposterous, even though she herself was dating other people.

I ended up in two of Chandler's classes, and it seemed as natural a thing in the world that Chandler and I would end up studying together. And even more natural that one night Chandler would lean over and kiss me just like he used to almost three years before.

He pulled back right away, and then just stared at me. "You know what's happened, don't you?" His eyes were so blue. "I've fallen in love with you all over again. I can see now it's you and me. It always has been."

My heart was pounding so hard I could hardly say what had to be said. "But, Chandler, what about Jenelle?"

His face reddened, and he said, "I realize now that was just an infatuation." He looked away and added, his voice real low, "I been hearing things about Jenelle for a long time now. You know how folks in Bullitt Lick love to spread bad news."

So he'd heard about Jenelle's running around, after all. I hadn't had to say a word. "I guess maybe I'm old-fashioned," Chandler went on, "but I need a wife who'll be faithful." He reached over and took my hand. "I need you, Ida Sue. You and I—well, we've got so much in common. We belong together."

He ran his hands through his hair and added, "It's going to be hard telling Jenelle. But it's got to be done."

I started feeling real hot, just thinking about it, wondering how Jenelle would take it. But Chandler said, "Don't worry. She'll understand. You'll see. She'll realize you and I were meant for each other."

Jenelle was waiting for Chandler on the front porch

when we went home for Christmas that year. When she lifted her hand to wave at him, I could see that diamond on her finger sparkling in the cold winter sun.

Jenelle's smile faded as soon as she saw me get out of the car, too. "Why, Ida Sue, I didn't know you were driving back with Chandler. I thought you might take the bus—" Her voice trailed off when she got a good look at our faces. I guess what we had to tell her was written all over them because Jenelle's face went chalky white. "What is going on?" Her voice went so loud and shrill that it brought Pa to the front door in back of her.

Chandler plunged right in, though. "I'm real sorry, Jenelle, but I've found out I love Ida Sue here. I always have." He went on, saying how he wouldn't hurt her for the world, but it was surely a lot kinder just to tell her outright than to lead her on.

I was watching Jenelle's face while Chandler talked. As pale as it was before, it went slowly deep, deep red.

"I know you'll wish us well," Chandler finished. I'll never forget what he looked like at that moment. So sweet, so earnest, so sure that this was the best way to handle everything.

Jenelle looked like she might faint. She swayed on her feet, and Chandler rushed forward to catch her. Jenelle started to speak, and for a second not a sound came out of her mouth. Then it was like a wail, the wail of an animal, wounded and hurting. "No-o-o-o." That was all she said. But she flung herself at Chandler, wrapped herself around him, as if she never meant to let go.

I knew right then what was happening. I'd seen her

eyes, like something was smoldering in them. "Chandler!" I yelled. "Get away from her!"

Chandler turned to me, his face registering surprise; and it seemed suddenly as if everything was happening in slow motion. Chandler made a move as if to pull away, but it was already too late. He opened his mouth to scream, and then they were both engulfed by a blue flame. A blue flame that burned and burned and burned—but didn't seem to ignite anything else. Nothing else but my sister and the man I loved.

I stood there, watching those awful flames, and it felt like a part of me was dying, too. Even from where I stood, a good three feet away, the heat was so intense I had to step back. I realized dimly that Pa had rushed outside, screaming Jenelle's name. Over and over he screamed it until it was just a whimper.

Then Pa turned to me. I can't forget what he said. "WHAT HAVE YOU DONE?" I keep hearing Pa say that. Over and over.

It's hard to believe, sitting out here, that this is where Jenelle and Chandler both died. Out here on this very porch. The floorboards aren't even singed.

Pa is still whimpering out in the kitchen. Still sniffling. I heard Pa telling everybody at the funeral and all those reporters that showed up that what happened was a terrible accident. That Jenelle didn't mean to do what she did. And that she sure didn't mean to take Chandler with her. I know that's a lie.

If Pa had seen what I saw that day, he'd know it, too. In the midst of the flames, for just a moment, I could still see

Jenelle's face. She was looking straight at me. And smiling that little half-smile. Until the flames rose so high, so hot, you couldn't see anything. Only her and Chandler's shapes, looking as if they were whirling in the blaze. Jenelle took Chandler from me on purpose. The only way she could, anymore.

It makes me so mad to think about it. But there's no one left to be mad at anymore. Nobody left to vent this awful anger on. I'm sitting out here, trying to cool down, trying to put it all into perspective. But the whole thing makes me so horribly mad. And Pa's sniffling out there keeps making me madder. And madder. I feel like I could just explode.

A Tale Told at Dusk

JACK KELLY

"Hey, boy, you ever seen a ghost? Now I don't mean one of them fellas with a sheet over his head. I mean somebody that ain't no longer there but you see them just like they was.

"Sometimes I see your mama like that. Especially in the evenings when I'm kind of tired, I'll see her walking up the lane or doing the chores around the house. Sometimes she'll come out on the porch there like she used to and be waiting for me to come in from milking the cows or be calling you in to supper or just be staring down towards the meadow like she was trying to see something real far away."

The day was relaxing into evening around the shabby

farmhouse and a few distant crickets began to take the pulse of night. They both leaned on the big oak that shaded the side yard, the man standing, his son sitting with his legs drawn up. Beneath the farmer's leathery face there was a certain pallor. His sharp squinting eyes flicked around as he spoke, as if they itched. The boy's face was an unfinished carving of his father's, with the deep lines and knots of pain only hinted at. The man spoke in a coarse, low-pitched drawl. Often he had to stop and swallow or clear his throat before he could continue.

"'Course I know that ain't really her 'cause she's dead, and it ain't even her spirit 'cause that's in heaven. A person's spirit don't hang around after they're dead, I know that. But it's like my eyes got so used to seeing her they just can't believe she's gone.

"Son, I know you been pretty miserable ever since the accident. God knows I been feeling it myself real bad. But you can't go on moping like this. She wouldn't have wanted that. No, sir, she wanted you to go to college and make something out of yourself more than a plain old dirt farmer like me. She wouldn't have liked it if she thought you was going to sit around all day and sulk.

"'Course when a fella loses his mother that's always hard. You remember how I sat down and cried when your grandma passed away, and she'd led a full life. But if you let it affect you too much, then you ain't honoring her spirit. No matter how sad you feel you got to get on with things. Can't just sit."

The boy had hardly spoken to his father since the accident. He now sat breaking twigs and staring into the thickening gloom. The man knew the boy was considering his words deeply, but he wished the boy would speak his mind and not keep all the pain bottled up inside of him. That was really the heart of the problem, not just the mother's passing or the accident itself but that the boy had gotten so close-mouthed afterwards that his grief was getting to be unnatural. The man wished there were some way he could get through to the boy and uncork the lid so his soul wouldn't suffocate.

"Don't think I don't know how you feel, son. There was never nothing nor nobody that meant as much to me as your mama. Ever since the accident the whole world seems different to me without her around. And when I wake up in the morning I think to myself: Why should I get up? What's the use of it now? It seems like I can't find my blood no more. And whenever I seem to see her like I was telling you, a cold sweat comes over my insides."

The trees and the house were becoming black silhouettes against the sky. Darkness seeped up from the damp grass to thicken the twilight and the man had trouble making out the expression on the boy's face. But he felt that maybe he had touched the right chord, for the boy sat almost immobile as if in deep thought.

"You know what your mama would always say to me when times got rough and I started feeling real low? She'd say: Look 'em in the eye, honey. And that's what you got to do if you want to be a man. You got to look the world in the eye just like—"

The boy suddenly jerked his head up as if awakening from a dream. On the porch the image of his mother appeared just as his father had described it, peering into the dusk. She seemed to be calling him. He stood up and started towards the house.

Darkness poured from the ground. The man was startled, then confused. "Wait a minute, son. I just want to know what you think of these things. We ain't finished talking yet."

The man moved in front of his son, but the boy kept going. He walked straight towards the house as if his father wasn't even there.

"Tomorrow," his mother said as the boy mounted the porch steps, "you got to go up and clip the grass on your daddy's grave."

The
Black
Cat

LEE SOMERVILLE

She was an old cat, coal black, lean and ugly. Her right ear had been chewed and her old hide showed scars, but she had a regal look when she sat under the rosebushes in the plaza and surveyed us with yellow-green eyes.

If the witch cat had a name, we never knew it. Miss Tessie fed it, as she fed other strays. She even let the old cat sleep in her store in rainy weather. But mostly the cat slept under the rosebushes in our plaza in Caton City, Texas. We have a pretty little plaza here in the center of town. It has a fountain and a statue of a tired Confederate soldier facing north, ready to defend us from Northern invaders, and a bit of grass and lots of rosebushes.

Nobody dared to pet the old cat. People gave the cat scraps of bread and meat from hamburgers and hot dogs.

She accepted this placidly, as a queen accepts homage from peons. Now and then a stray dog came through our small dusty town, saw the cat, and made a lunge at it. The cat would retreat to the base of the fountain, turn, and lash with a razor-sharp claw that sliced the poor dog's nose. The dog would run howling while townspeople laughed. Our dogs, having learned the hard way, left that cat alone.

When I was fourteen, my mother's jailbird distant relative, Cousin Rush, came to live with us. My little brother Pete and I had to give up our room to this scruffy relative, but that wasn't the only reason I disliked him. I despised his dumpy figure and his smelly cigars and his scaly bald head and his way of looking at me with beady small eyes and nodding and winking.

Mama told me to show Cousin Rush the town, and I had to do it. This was the day before Halloween, and half the town was in the theater across the street from the plaza, rehearsing for the Heritage Festival we have every Halloween night. Miss Tessie was at the front of the theater, selling plastic masks of Cajun Caton and Davy Crockett. We have this play about Cajun Caton and a Delaware Indian, Chief Cut Hand, saving the town from Comanches on a Halloween night in the early 1800s. It ends with Cajun Caton, town hero, leaving his wife and eight children later on and going off with Davy Crockett and getting killed in the Alamo during the Texas Revolution against Mexico in 1836.

Cousin Rush bought a mask from Miss Tessie. He smiled and flirted and talked of the Importance of History.

His face smiled, but his eyes remained cold and scornful, and I could tell he thought this heritage business was hillbilly country foolishness. He'd already told me Caton City was a hick town filled with stupid people. It didn't compare with real towns.

As we started walking across the plaza, the black cat jumped from the rosebushes and ran in front of us.

To keep walking in a straight direction would have meant bad luck. I sidestepped and made a little circle. I'm not superstitious, not really, but no use taking chances.

Cousin Rush laughed at me. Then, to show his scorn of superstition and black cats, he did a fat-legged little hop and skip and kicked that cat in the stomach.

The old cat doubled up on Cousin Rush's sharp-toed shoe. She clawed at his sock, then bounced into a rosebush. She landed on her feet, stood there, weaving, hurt. Cousin Rush kicked again, and she dodged. She ran into the street, stopped, looked at Cousin Rush with yellow-green eyes. As he popped his hands together, making a threatening noise, she stood her ground for a moment, then ran into Miss Tessie's store.

"You didn't have to do that," I said.

Cousin Rush stood there, the October sun beating down on his bald head and his cigar sticking out of his fat face. "You country bumpkins don't have to act ignorant, but you do. The only way to deal with a black cat running across your path is to kick the manure out of the cat. It's a callous world, Brian, and the only way to deal with it is to skin your buddy before he skins you."

"We don't act that way here."

"You are fools." He blew cigar smoke and looked at the people milling around in front of the theater, talking and being friendly. "Now, tell me about this Heritage Festival you'll have tomorrow night. As I understand it, half the town is in the play, including the sheriff and his deputy. The other half—and that includes a lot of people that make this a sort of homecoming—will buy tickets and make cash contributions to the historical society. I understand this crazy old maid, this Miss Tessie, has collected a neat bit of cash."

"She's raising money for a historical marker to honor her ancestor, Cajun Caton."

"Yes. That's the idiot the town is named for."

"He was not an idiot. Caton and Davy Crockett were both killed in the Alamo, and they were Texas heroes."

Cousin Rush blew more smoke. "And there are at least a hundred people in this town descended from Caton. I understand that during the finale of this play, which Miss Tessie wrote, it has become a custom for every man in the audience to put on a mask to honor Cajun Caton or Davy Crockett? Hmmm."

I didn't like the sudden suspicion I had. I'd heard Mama and Dad talking in whispers, telling that Rush had served time in a Texas penitentiary for small-time robbery. I didn't like the cold, greedy look on my cousin's face.

I could have reported my suspicion to Sheriff Mitchell or to Deputy Haskins except for one thing—my mother was an Adams. Every Adams is intensely loyal to other Adamses, and don't you forget it. Cousin Rush was Rushid E. Sarosy, and his daddy had been a shoe salesman in Dallas, but his mama was Verney Adams to start with.

Verney was a hot little blonde who was born with a female urge and grew up around it. She left Caton County fifty-six years ago for the big city, but she was still an Adams.

I had a suspicion, from the calculating look on his face, that Cousin Rush would burgle some place tomorrow night when everybody was in the theater, or he'd rob the box office at the theater, wearing a mask like everybody else would wear.

I couldn't talk to Mama about my suspicions. If I was wrong and Cousin Rush didn't do anything bad, she'd say I was disloyal to the name of Adams.

As we left the plaza, the old black cat that Cousin Rush had kicked came out of Miss Tessie's store and looked at us as if it were casting a spell. I shivered.

I still wonder if what happened that night was just coincidence.

My little brother Pete had been unsuccessfully baiting an animal trap for a week. The trap was in the backyard. Here in Caton City, which is in northeast Texas, just south of Oklahoma and not far from Arkansas between the Red River and the Sulphur River, things were different. Coyotes and raccoons and possums and other animals came into town at night to raid garbage cans. Pete had been baiting that animal trap, actually a cage, for a week with cornbread, beans, cabbage, and such, hoping to catch a raccoon and make a pet of it. On this night, with a big moon beaming down, he had jerry-rigged a Rube Goldberg device that would turn on a light if the trap door was triggered.

Cousin Rush had our room now, so we slept in beds on

our big screened-in back porch. About midnight the signal light came on to show the trap door had slammed down. Pete got out of bed in his underwear and ran barefoot to the trap, waving a flashlight.

He came back in a hurry. "Brian, we got trouble!"

I sat up, sniffed. "I smell it." The smell of skunk was not all that strong, showing the animal was fairly content, but it was definitely skunk.

"You got to shoot it."

"Heck, no! If you shoot that skunk, it'll make a smell that will wake up the town," I cautioned. "It has plenty of food and water and room to move around in that cage-trap. After it eats, it will probably go to sleep, won't it?"

Pete thought this over. "I guess so, unless it's disturbed."

"Okay. I'll make sure the yard gates are closed, so no dogs or other animals can disturb that skunk. We'll figure what to do after it gets daylight tomorrow. Let sleeping skunks sleep, that's my motto."

After Pete had gone back to bed, I lay awake, thinking. I could take a long fishing pole, hold the cage as far from me as possible, and move gently. I'd have to get that skunk out of our backyard somehow. . . .

I finally went to sleep and dreamed that Cousin Rush robbed Miss Tessie of all the Heritage Festival money. He got by with it because he was wearing a mask and all the men in the crowd he joined afterward wore masks. Nobody knew which masked man had the money. I woke up. Then I went to sleep again and this time I dreamed Cousin Rush didn't get away with it after all. He came out of the theater with the money still in his hands, and the old black cat cast a spell on him and made him throw the money in the air.

And I dreamed the old cat was really a witch in disguise.

When I woke up, it was Halloween Day and I still didn't know what to do about Cousin Rush. Maybe I was suspicious of him because I didn't like him.

But later in the day, as I listened to him talk with Miss Tessie, I became more alarmed. Oh, it was just general talk, discussion of the fact that Cajun Caton wasn't really a Cajun. He was from Henry County, Tennessee, and he had picked up that nickname in Louisiana in what Miss Tessie described as an "indiscreet house."

I watched as Cousin Rush got his Oldsmobile filled with gas and the tires and oil checked. Looked like he was planning for a trip. He couldn't go to Houston, because police would arrest him if he went back there. He'd had trouble with his fourth wife in Dallas, and was wanted on charges there. But the way he was fussing around his car, it looked as if he would go somewhere in a hurry.

Long before the Heritage Play started that night, he parked his car on the north side of the plaza near the biggest rosebush. Then he went into the theater early, carrying a cape and a mask as some other men were doing.

I stood looking across the plaza, worried. The black cat came from the rosebushes, sat on the base of the fountain, and stared back at me. Darkness came, and a full moon rose. Stars shone.

Looking at that cat, I knew what I had to do. Maybe it wouldn't work, but maybe it would. I had to try.

After the play was well under way, with everyone except me in the theater, I got a long fishing pole and some cord. Cautiously, holding my breath at times, I carried that animal cage-trap the three blocks to the plaza. The skunk, his belly full of cornbread and cabbage and beans, slept most of the time.

I learned later that during the last two minutes of the play a man wearing a mask and a cape went inside the box office where Miss Tessie was counting money. He didn't speak a word, but he pushed a small pistol in Miss Tessie's face and motioned for her to sit down. He tied her to the chair. She opened her mouth to scream, and he jammed a handkerchief in it. Nobody would have heard if she had screamed because the audience and the cast were singing the finale.

The man put his pistol inside his cape, took handfuls of the paper money she'd been sorting. He stuffed money in his pockets and inside the cape pockets, and left with some money in his hands.

He walked out of the theater as the townspeople, wearing capes and masks, also walked out.

I knew which one was Cousin Rush. I could tell by the prissy walk and the dumpy figure.

A couple of kids ran ahead of him across the plaza, but I pulled the cord I had rigged to the trap door. With that door open, and with all the noise, the skunk would come out. He would not be disturbed or afraid, because skunks are not usually afraid. Even a grizzly bear would tippity-toe around a skunk.

The two kids apparently saw him, hollered, "Uh-oh,"

detoured slightly, and kept running. Cousin Rush paid them no attention.

Then Miss Tessie's old black cat ran out of the rosebushes, ran right in front of Cousin Rush, and ran back into the bushes.

Cousin Rush slowed in his fast walk to the Oldsmobile. It was a beautiful night, bright as day with white moonlight and black shadows. Just as Cousin Rush got near his car, a small black animal came out of the rosebushes again, right in front of him.

If he had climbed in his car without noticing, he would have gotten away with robbery. Being Cousin Rush and being naturally mean, and probably thinking this was Miss Tessie's old black cat, he kicked the skunk.

Then he bent over, ready to kick again. He got that spray full in his face. He staggered back, threw both arms in the air, hands spread wide. Money fluttered high, caught the wind, and blew all over the plaza. Cousin Rush fought for breath, ran into the monument, bounced off, stumbled against the fountain, coughed, gasped, vomited, and waved his hands again.

He tore off his mask and cape, and money came from the pockets inside the cape and swirled in the air. People stood watching, wondering.

Somebody found Miss Tessie bound and gagged and cut her loose. She ran into the street, screaming she'd been robbed.

With all those dollar bills and five dollar bills and ten dollar bills floating in the air around Cousin Rush, he became the Prime Suspect. Nobody went near him for a while, though. The smell was nauseating.

Finally Sheriff Mitchell spoke firm words to Deputy Haskins. Haskins looked reluctant, but Mitchell gave the orders. Don't take him to our clean jail, he said. Take him to the old county stables and lock him up for the night.

The skunk got away in all the excitement. Nobody would have touched him anyway. I knew I had to pick up the cage-trap when everybody left, or I'd be incriminated. I didn't want Mama to know I'd had anything to do with trapping Cousin Rush.

Citizens picked up the money that was blowing around and put it in a well-ventilated place for the night. Then people left for the American Legion Barbecue and Dance. Some of those who had gotten close to skunk smell while picking up the money might have to stay outside the Legion Hall, but they'd eat and drink and they'd survive.

As the crowd left the plaza, and as Deputy Haskins started Cousin Rush walking twenty feet ahead of him to the stables, I saw Miss Tessie's old black cat sitting on the base of the fountain. Her eyes glinted in the Halloween moonlight, and I'll swear that cat was laughing.

The Balancing Man

CHARLES ARDAI

I was eleven when my brother Friendly took me to see the balancing man.

The day we went was a hot spring Wednesday, the kind when it can be three o'clock but the sweat in you thinks it's high noon. Friendly and I were slacking off behind the heaven elm in the school courtyard, lazing in its shade and putting off going back inside as long as we could. School was no place to be on a day like this. Anyone with half a brain could see that, Friendly said.

It wasn't long before it became too late for us to go to class with an excuse about forgetting what time it was—exactly when we passed the point of no return I can't say, but at one point we both knew that we had. The only thing keeping us where we were then was the shade of that towering elm . . . but it was hardly the only tree around. So we got to our feet and stepped out into the sun, crimping our eyes shut and wiping our necks and foreheads as trickles of sweat started bubbling up.

We dashed up over Morton's Hill and into the wilds at the edge of the school grounds, plunging through the forest and changing course to meet any big tree we saw, among whose roots we could spend a few minutes lying around and breathing in the scent of the damp earth. Friendly climbed some trees, too, because that's the sort of thing he liked to do; as for me, I like the ground and was more than happy to stay on it.

For a while our path kept us in sight of the schoolyard— we ducked into the undergrowth and held our breaths whenever we thought someone in the yard was looking our way—but pretty soon we'd wandered far enough to be completely lost. Luckily, Friendly had a good sense of direction and he was able to tell where we had gotten to just by looking at the moss on the trees or something like that. I trusted him and he trusted himself; so we kept on walking and whistling and sitting under trees until we came to a path and I realized that we hadn't just been wandering, we had been heading somewhere.

I was a little peeved that Friendly had known all along where we were going. The whole point of wandering is not having to get somewhere, and knowing that we'd had a goal all along took away some of the fun.

"Ted," Friendly said when I told him this, "you don't know anything. Where we're going's better than just wandering. You'll see." And that took care of that, because when Friendly said something like that, he meant it.

We went down the path till it crossed Tocolow Road, then took a shortcut through someone's property and over an old wood bridge. Eventually we found ourselves on another dirt path, this one even narrower than the first. It looked like a driveway someone had started and then abandoned when he decided not to bother building a house after all. Sure enough, where the path ended there was no house, just a cleared area and a tall red wood barn.

No house, but a barn? Friendly was right. This was interesting.

"Now, listen," he told me. He bent over with his hands on his knees even though I was almost as tall as he was. I bent over, too, so he could whisper in my ear. "You've got to do exactly as I say. Okay?"

I nodded.

"When we go inside," he said, "you can't talk. You can't make any noise at all. You understand?"

I nodded.

"And when I pull on your arm like this"—he tugged on one of my sleeves—"you just follow me out. Got that?"

I nodded. Friendly straightened up and started off down the path, but I ran after him and caught one of his belt loops. He spun around.

"Friendly, what's inside?" I said.

He clamped his hand over my mouth and darted glances left and right. "Shhh!"

I tried to talk through his hand but couldn't make a sound, so I licked his palm. He jerked it away and wiped it on his jeans. This time I whispered.

"Friendly, what's in there?"

"You'll see," he said. "Come on."

He pulled me toward the barn. As we got closer, he slouched down a little and took his steps more slowly, careful not to make a sound. I did the same.

We ran out of path about five yards short of the barn, and from there I could see that the doors were already open a little. I wondered if Friendly had known they would be, and if so how, but I had promised not to talk, so I didn't. Friendly crept up to the doors and stuck his head in, then waved his hand for me to join him. I went as quietly as I could, though when I reached Friendly's side he frowned in a way that told me I had made too much noise. He put his finger to his lips again, stepped through the door, and pulled me inside by my shirt collar.

I must have looked completely confused—I remember that my eyes opened so wide they hurt—because Friendly broke his own rule. He stuck his mouth right up against my ear and hissed, *"It's the balancing man."*

It certainly was.

The inside of the barn was hollowed out: no stables, no loft, no troughs, nothing you'd expect to find in a barn. But it wasn't empty. It was the farthest thing from empty. It was full. Only it wasn't full of anything that made sense.

It was full of trestles and sawhorses, pewter cooking pots and lacquered settees, long dangling hanks of rope and window shutters and automobile doors. It was full of garden hoses, long canvas mail sacks, and a jackhammer. It was full of television antennas and serving platters.

Right in front of us, perched on a pair of cinder blocks, there was a refrigerator, turned over on its side. On top of the refrigerator there was a hat stand, and wedged on top of the hat stand was an extension ladder stretched out horizontally to its full length of ten feet or so. At either end, the ladder was strung with lengths of copper wire; the wire went straight up for maybe twenty feet, where it was looped on one side around a pair of umbrellas and on the other around a metal statue of a baseball player. I can't tell you what the umbrellas and the statue were connected to since that would just bring up the same question again and it would all take too long in the telling; but I'll tell you, looking around the barn I saw more *things,* connected up in more ways, than I'd ever seen before.

There was a grandfather clock with its pendulum missing dangling high overhead. There was a set of golf clubs roped together to prop up an upended washbasin. There was a well bucket tied to the end of a long, colorful scarf. There was a tambourine. There was a box of crackers. Anything you'd care to name was in there somewhere.

All this stuff was piled up like a mighty ziggurat, only instead of coming to a point at the top, it came to maybe a dozen points, each sticking out like a turret from a castle. The turrets were tied to each other with thick cables of wire, like tightropes in the circus. On one of these cables I could see a lemon crate, and sticking out of the lemon crate there was a sword, and balanced on the pommel of the sword there was a bicycle seat. Squatting on the bicycle seat, forty feet up, was an old man.

He sat, and he looked straight ahead, and he seemed not

to notice the extremely perilous position he was in. For although the structure had outcroppings in every possible direction and at every possible location, he had chosen the one spot I could see where a slip would be certain to pitch him the whole forty feet to the ground.

It was something like watching an act in the circus, except that nothing happened. The man sat, and he sat, and he didn't budge, and though I couldn't tell from so far below, I wouldn't have been surprised to learn that he wasn't even blinking. I remember thinking that if *I* were perched on a bicycle seat, on a sword, on a lemon crate, on a high wire, I wouldn't budge either.

I looked away from the man, away from the huge tower of odds and ends, at the only spot of sense my eyes could find: my own shoes. But no sooner had my head stopped spinning a little than Friendly was tugging on my sleeve. My first thought was that we were leaving, but when I looked up I saw that Friendly was pointing. The man now had his hands pressed down on the bicycle seat with his long legs extended out to either side of him. As I watched, he turned himself over entirely, resting the top of his head on the bicycle seat and curling his arms around his chest and his legs around each other.

Then he didn't budge again for the longest time.

I didn't want to stay. I was frightened for the old man; he was sure to fall and I didn't want to see it happen. So I tugged on Friendly's sleeve and pleaded with him silently.

He ignored me and started walking around the base of the ziggurat, poking a finger in here, staring through a gap there. I wished that he would stop, but there didn't seem to be anything I could do to make him. I followed him around the wall of the barn, once or twice glancing up and then glancing down again quickly.

When we reached the side of the barn opposite where we had come in, I saw three other kids already there, huddled in the shadows, watching the balancing man. I looked at the three boys closely, but I didn't recognize them. They looked about my brother's age or maybe a little bit older.

They made room for us on the floor. Friendly sat down, so I had to, too. They all looked up with big smiles on their faces, as though there were a giant television screen under the roof and it was showing their favorite program.

The balancing man was still standing on his head, and it was then that I realized just how old he was. His beard hung down at least two feet in front of his face, long and off-white, the color that curtains get if you don't wash them very often. He was wearing a black turtleneck shirt and a black vest with black trousers, but because of his position I could see bits of his arms and legs, which were very thin: he looked like a doll made out of straw.

But he must have been strong! Stronger than anyone in the world, to be able to balance the way he did! And more than strong; he must have been . . . I couldn't think of the word I wanted. Today, I think of the word "agile," but that falls so far short of describing this extraordinary man that I think I was better off when I couldn't think of a word at all. I was amazed, and more than amazed: I was shocked. I was impressed. I was frightened. And I was embarrassed for watching, for Friendly and the other boys' gawking. I knew now, from the way Friendly had spoken, that this wasn't the first time he had come here.

At least the balancing man didn't seem to know we were there; I was glad about that. But I was also terrified. What if one of us should bump into something, or stick his finger where it didn't belong? It would be a tragedy.

I closed my eyes and pressed my chin to my chest and didn't look up again even when Friendly tapped on my shoulder and tried to lift my chin. I didn't open my eyes until Friendly hissed in my ear, "Okay, come on!"

The other three boys were already halfway to the door and Friendly was edging in that direction. I went with him. Still, I couldn't resist the urge to look up once more, and when I didn't see the balancing man on the crate my heart leapt up into my throat. Then I caught sight of him only a few feet away, walking easily along another of the cables. His stride was long and brave, and so perfectly composed—he even had his hands in his pockets!—that I felt sure for a moment that walking on a wire must be the most natural thing on earth for him. He had such an air of unconcern about him that I felt as though my amazement at his performance was somehow unwarranted. How much of a fool would I have thought someone who had praised my ability to lie in bed without falling out, or to comb my hair without putting out an eye?

My head swam with confusion and I was so relieved when we reached the door that I ran through it and down the driveway without waiting for Friendly.

I didn't run far, though, and Friendly caught up with me quickly. We sat down together in the woods. He looked at me with a sort of sly pride in his face, as though he had just initiated me into some delicious, illicit pleasure.

"So? What'd you think?"

I shook my head. It didn't help. "Who is he?" I asked.

"Who cares?" Friendly said. "He's some guy. He's a nut. He's an alien from outer space. What difference does it make? He's just someone. What do you think?"

"I don't get it."

Friendly laughed and lay back against the root of a tree. "Nope, I bet you don't."

"Do *you*?" If anyone understood this, I was sure it would be Friendly.

"Sure," he said. "The man's a loony tune."

"But how does he do it?" I asked.

"How? He probably collects up junk from around here. Maybe he steals things."

"No, I mean how does he . . . balance?"

Friendly shrugged. Then he said very quietly, "I hear that crazy people are twelve times stronger than normal people."

"Really?"

Friendly nodded. Then he sat up and put his hands on my shoulders. "You can't tell anyone about this," he said. "Especially Mom and Dad. You understand?"

I nodded.

"Good." He ruffled my hair and stood up, brushing soil off his jeans. "Now let's go home."

It wasn't easy, but as Friendly led me home, I forced myself to remember the path we took.

* * *

The second time I went by myself. It was a Saturday, and I told everyone that I was going to meet Jesse at his house. I told Jesse, too, and he said he'd cover for me.

This time the barn doors were closed, but they still weren't locked. I opened them gently, just far enough for me to squeeze in. To make sure that I was alone I walked all the way around the barn. I was.

Then I looked for the balancing man, but I couldn't see him—it was still too early in the day for much light to come in through the windows. I stood where I was and I waited, and in a while my eyes adjusted until I could make out the old man's shape up on the highest point of the tower.

Both of his feet were crowded onto the top of what was either a basketball or a volleyball. The ball itself was perched at one end of a steep wooden plank and I couldn't see why it didn't roll down and take him with it.

In one hand he had what looked like a metal coffeepot and he was using it to water some plants that were growing out of a porcelain bathtub. When he was done, he set the pot down on the edge of the bathtub and turned completely around with a single, sudden twist of his torso. The ball started to carry him down the incline, slowly at first, then at a tremendous rate. At the end of the plank there was a circular hole through which the ball dropped into a net—but the balancing man sailed off the end of the platform, aimed right at the wall of the barn.

As he flew, he stretched one of his arms out behind him and snagged an upright flagpole, which whipped him around in a half circle and deposited him on a small wooden platform a few feet below. My heart very generously started beating again.

I had to fight a strong urge to run away. I wasn't even sure why I had come. Crazy people were twelve times stronger than regular people, after all—of which strength I had just seen a fine demonstration—so I was scared.

But there are some things in life which you can't just see once and pass over without questioning. There are some bits of food which are too big to swallow unchewed. I wasn't like Friendly, who could see the balancing man and think only of his own entertainment. What I didn't realize until much later is that people like Friendly are, perhaps, to be envied.

I waited until the balancing man was balanced steadily on his bicycle seat and then I said, "Good morning." I didn't want to startle him—I certainly didn't want him to fall—but somehow I was confident that I wouldn't and he wouldn't. I spoke loudly, but not suddenly.

He looked down and I could almost see him straining to make me out. "Good morning," he said.

His voice was small and distant, which was not a surprise. But it was also clear and deep, with none of the taints that age so often brings. He did not seem disturbed by my presence.

"My name is Ted," I said, a little louder.

"Mine isn't," he said.

"What is your name?" I asked. He didn't answer. This he didn't seem to have heard.

I cupped my hands around my mouth and shouted: "What are you doing up there?"

"I'm balancing," he said.

"But why?" I asked.

"Because if I didn't balance," he said, "I'd fall."

He slid off his perch and sat down on the cable, his skinny legs dangling over the edge.

"Why don't you come down?" I shouted.

"Why don't you come up?" he said.

I didn't know what to say. "Because I don't know how! I wouldn't be safe! I'd fall!"

"Exactly," the balancing man said. As though this was his reason, too.

"Don't you *ever* come down?" I said.

"No. It's dangerous."

I waved my arm at the structure beneath him. "Where did this come from?"

"Where did that come from?" The balancing man pointed out one of the windows. "Where did you come from?"

"I came from home," I said. "I wanted to know if you needed any help."

For a long time he didn't speak. I began to think he wasn't going to. Then he said, "No, you didn't. You don't understand me. You are afraid of me. That's why you came."

It was, more or less, the truth.

"The feeling," he said, and here his voice trembled a little, "is mutual."

"What does that mean?" I asked.

"It means, young man, that I am afraid of you."

"Of me?"

"No," the balancing man said. "Of *you*."

"I don't understand—"

"Please," the old man said suddenly. "Leave me alone."

I was surprised at this and a little bit hurt. Neither of us moved for a good five minutes, and then I lowered my head and walked out. I did not go back.

Friendly did go back. I couldn't stop him. In all honesty, I didn't try; but it wouldn't have mattered if I had. It was a hangout for those kids we had seen there and a couple of others. (Friendly told me names, but I've forgotten them, if I ever remembered.) They were his friends now, and you could have made him give up his own family before you'd have gotten him to stop going to that barn.

Once he asked me to go with him again; when I refused, he made fun of me. Another time he tried to take me there without telling me where we were going, like the first time, but I got wise when we hit Tocolow Road and I screamed at him like I had the devil in me. I said I'd tell Mom and Dad. He told me to go to hell then, that he'd stab me in my sleep if I did any such thing. Friendly and I didn't talk much after that day.

But I knew he kept going back because it showed in his face, the way it would show when he had his hands behind his back in the wintertime and you could just *tell* that he had a snowball he was about to throw. He had a secret, and he wanted it to stay that way, but part of him wanted to shout it out to the world: *I'm Friendly Cooper and have I got something to tell you!* That was the part that showed in his face.

And sometimes it wasn't even a matter of reading his

face. Sometimes he'd just come right out and tell me, almost like he was daring me to do something about it. He told me when they snuck eight people in there at once— *and the guy didn't notice a thing! What do you think of that, Ted?* He told me when Martin, or Mark, or someone, burped real loud and someone else laughed, *but that guy must be blind, or deaf maybe, 'cause you could see he didn't hear a thing!* He told me the day one of them climbed up on top of the refrigerator and sat on it—*and then he got down real quick, but nothing happened, the guy didn't notice.* So of course they all had to do it. And then, of course, someone climbed a little higher.

And then one afternoon Friendly came home glowering, his eyes set in furious determination, his breathing deliberate like a bull's when he's led into the ring. Martin had climbed up past the refrigerator, Friendly said, over the ladder, through the barrel, and up over the automobile tires when that old monster came up behind him and kicked him off. He just *kicked* him off. He put his foot on Martin's back and pushed, and the whole stack of tires fell and Martin fell with them, maybe fifteen feet. The others picked him up because he couldn't walk, and they beat it the hell out of there. When they got to Martin's house, they told his mother he'd fallen out of a tree. She took him to a doctor in Port and the doctor said his leg was broke clean through.

Friendly's face was white with terror and red with shame and black with anger as he told me this. Until you see a face like that you can't imagine what it looks like. I hope you never do.

I never have since, except that I've seen it quite a lot in my dreams. Usually it's superimposed over a headline from the Gavin County *Dispatch*. The paper's dated a week later and the headline says

FIRE DESTROYS TWO ACRES

and the story tells how the volunteer fire department managed to contain a potentially devastating fire on one small plot of land. The story is basically an upbeat one, and why not? No one lived on that land; it was just being used as a dumping ground by people in the area, judging by the burned-up junk the firemen found at the center of the blaze. And the firemen got there in time to put it out before it spread. A happy day all around.

If I'm lucky, the dream stops there—I wake up sweating into my sheets like I'm under a heat lamp and my heart's beating so hard my ribs ache, but at least I'm awake. Then there are the other nights, the ones when the dream goes on the same as it did the first time, when I was eleven years old and sleeping right down the hall from my parents.

Sometimes Friendly's in it, sometimes he's not. Sometimes I'm in it. Sometimes I pour the gasoline and light the match. But the part that's always the same is what comes next, after the boys all run away.

Flames bite into the walls of the barn, climb gently, slowly up toward the roof, lighting the red wood a fine, smoldering orange. And as the flames climb, a spark catches here, on the wooden stave of a barrel, a spark catches there, on the fringes of a scarf held up with clothespins.

The old man squats on his bicycle seat, on the sword, on

the lemon crate, on the high wire, forty feet up, and he doesn't notice right away. Then he smells something; then he glimpses the first flames; then he sees the barrel collapse onto itself, all flame and ashes, the scarf curl up and blacken in an instant.

He jumps off the seat onto the cable, and the crate, the sword, and the seat fall the forty feet and smash on the floor. He sees more flames: in front of him, so he turns around, but they're behind him, too. He shimmies up a wire, climbs over some boxes, and then the flame's under him, slapping hungry tongues against his feet. Soft metals melt, wood burns, cloth vanishes, and all the connections come apart one by one. A turret tips and falls. The cable snarls under his feet and he leaps to another cable, a higher plank, until he's all the way up by the bathtub with his plants.

At this point, the dream can go one of two ways, depending on whether the plank he's standing on burns up quickly enough or the roof collapses, crushing him first.

If I'm lucky here, I wake up in tears. If I'm unlucky, I dream it all over again.

And you wonder, why? I said it myself, I couldn't have talked Friendly out of going; and even if I could have, the others would still have been there. Nothing would have been different. Maybe at eleven I'm entitled to a measure of irrational guilt, but at forty?

But you've got it wrong. It isn't guilt and it never has been. It's grief.

I'll be honest with you. I hadn't had this dream in a long time. Years. I hadn't thought about any of it in ages. The only reason it came back now is because of another headline I read, just last week:

WEEKEND RAMPAGE

It seems that some teenagers went into Central Park late last Saturday night, found a dozen homeless people sleeping in cardboard boxes, and set them on fire. Then they went home.

And I can't help but think about the old man on his high wire saying he was afraid not of me, but of *us*.

He had every reason to be.

Biographies

CATHLEEN JORDAN
(EDITOR)

Cathleen Jordan is the editor of *Alfred Hitchcock Mystery Magazine.* Raised in Fort Worth, Texas, she is a graduate of the University of Texas and holds an M.A. in English from the University of South Dakota. She is the author of *A Carol in the Dark,* a mystery novel. She and her husband live in New York City.

CHARLES ARDAI
THE BALANCING MAN

At age seventeen Charles Ardai sold his first short story to *Ellery Queen's Mystery Magazine.* Since then his stories, articles, and reviews have appeared in more than a dozen magazines and in such collections as *The Year's Best Horror Stories XIX* and *3rd Annual Best Mystery Stories of the Year,* an audio anthology. "The Balancing Man" is one of ten stories he has published to date in *Alfred Hitchcock Mystery Magazine.* He lives in New York City.

ELLIOTT CAPON
FUN AND GAMES AT THE WHACKS MUSEUM

Elliott Capon was born and reared in Brooklyn. He has a B.A. in English from the City University of New York. "Fun and Games at the Whacks Museum" is one of eight stories he has written for *Alfred Hitchcock Mystery Magazine,* starting with "Upon Reflection," a vampire story, published in 1985. He lives in suburban New Jersey with his wife and son.

NINA KIRIKI HOFFMAN
POURING THE FOUNDATIONS OF A NIGHTMARE

Nina Kiriki Hoffman's short fiction has appeared in *Alfred Hitchcock Mystery Magazine, Weird Tales, Amazing Stories, Asimov's Science Fiction, The Magazine of Fantasy and Science Fiction, Analog, Pulphouse,* and elsewhere, including in several "Year's Best" anthologies. She is the author of *The Thread That Binds the Bones,* and she collaborated with Tad Williams on *Child of an Ancient City.* She has lived in, and set stories in, California, Idaho, and Oregon.

THEODORE H. HOFFMAN
SITTER

Ted Hoffman is a journalist specializing in the arts for a Northern California newspaper. He holds a B.A. in film from the University of South Florida. He is the founder of a fiction writers' group called Write On!, and in 1988 won a regional stand-up comedy competition in Tampa, Florida. "Sitter" was his second published short story.

JACK KELLY
A TALE TOLD AT DUSK

Jack Kelly lives in Milan, New York. He has worked as a lifeguard, taxi driver, ambulance attendant, screenwriter, and designer of water pistols. His latest novel is *Mad Dog*, about the career of bank robber John Dillinger.

ANN MACKENZIE
I CAN'T HELP SAYING GOODBYE

Ann Mackenzie, mother of five and grandmother of six, has lived in most countries in southern Africa with her geologist husband. They have now settled—permanently, they hope—in Johannesburg, where they run the Gem Education Centre. Children feature more prominently than gemstones in Ms. Mackenzie's many published short stories—especially rather strange and different children, like the little girl in the story included here.

TAYLOR MCCAFFERTY
OLD FLAME

An identical twin, Taylor McCafferty was born and brought up in Louisville, Kentucky. She was graduated magna cum laude from the University of Louisville and worked as an art director and advertising copywriter for a

Louisville ad agency. She has three children. Her first novel, *Pet Peeves,* introduced Haskell Blevins, the only private detective in the fictional small town of Pigeon Fork, Kentucky. The fourth book in this series, *Thin Skins,* has just been published. She is also the author of a new mystery, *Heir Condition,* under the pseudonym Tierney McClellan. Her short fiction has appeared in *Redbook* and *Alfred Hitchcock Mystery Magazine.*

OGDEN NASH
THE THREE D'S

Ogden Nash was born in Rye, New York, in 1902 and died in 1971. During his lifetime he produced quantities of mostly light, satirical verse; he is known for his unorthodox style and rhymes and for his delightful wit. His more than two dozen books of poetry and prose include *I'm a Stranger Here Myself* (1938), *Versus* (1949), *You Can't Get There from Here* (1957), *and Everyone but Thee and Me* (1962). With S. J. Perelman he wrote the libretto for Kurt Weill's *One Touch of Venus.* Most of his poetry was first published in *The New Yorker,* the magazine that bought his first poem, "Spring Comes to Murray Hill," in 1931.

ARTHUR PORGES
PUDDLE

Arthur Porges was born in 1915 in Chicago. He holds a B.S. and an M.S. from the Illinois Institute of Technology in mathematics, and taught college math for about fifteen years, with a hiatus for army service from 1942 to 1945.

In 1957 he stopped teaching to write full time. He has sold more than 250 stories to national magazines, mostly in the science fiction and detective story genres, as well as many essays, some poems, and a few mathematical pieces. Many of his stories have been used abroad on radio and television; "The Ruum" has been reprinted more than twenty-five times. He is the author of *Three Porges Parodies and a Pastiche,* a collection of Sherlock Holmes takeoffs.

ALAN RYAN
THE WITCH, THE CHILD, AND THE U.P.S. FELLOW

Alan Ryan is the author of four novels and two volumes of short stories, and has edited seven anthologies. He has served as vice president of the National Book Critics Circle and is a frequent contributor to *USA Today,* the *Washington Post, New York Newsday,* the *Atlanta Journal,* and a wide variety of other newspapers and magazines. Understandably, he says, he sometimes gets silly.

LEE SOMERVILLE
THE BLACK CAT

Lee Somerville sold his first magazine story when he was a fourteen-year-old farm boy in 1929. Since then he has sold more than 200 short stories, and twice that many articles, to magazines. One of his novels, *Charge of the Model T's,* became a 1977 movie starring Louis Nye and Arte Johnson. Colonel Somerville has been a high school principal, a basketball coach, and a university teacher. He enlisted in the army in World War II, where he was a rifleman in an infantry company. On his retirement some years later he was a combat crew commander in Atlas-F Intercontinental Missiles with the rank of lieutenant colonel, U.S. Air Force. He and his wife, Emily, live in Paris, Texas, and own a Red River County ranch.

MAGGIE WAGNER-HANKINS
WITCH AND COUSIN

Maggie Wagner-Hankins has been writing fiction for as long as she can remember. Her fascination with the supernatural, mystical side of life has influenced much of her work. Her stories have appeared in many adult, young adult, and children's publications including *Alfred Hitchcock Mystery Magazine* and *YM*. More recent probings into women's issues and nature-based spirituality have marked her latest works, including her most recent young adult novel, *Cicada*. She makes her home in Missouri with her daughter Celia and their kitten, Smudge.

CHET WILLIAMSON
THE UNDERTAKER'S WEDDING

Chet Williamson is the author of a number of horror and mystery novels, including *Ash Wednesday, Lowland Rider, McKain's Dilemma,* and *Soulstorm.* His short fiction has appeared in *The New Yorker* and *Playboy* as well as in a wide variety of science fiction, horror, and mystery magazines and anthologies. He lives in Elizabethtown, Pennsylvania, with his wife and son.